THE CORONA BOOK OF
GHOST STORIES

Also available

THE CORONA BOOK OF
GHOST
STORIES

edited by
SUE J. EATON

First published in the United Kingdom in 2019
1

by Corona Books UK
www.coronabooks.com

ISBN 978-1-9996579-5-6

Cover design by Martin Bushell
www.creatusadvertising.co.uk

CONTENTS

INTRODUCTION

Whatever your views on ghosts, and I expect you have some one way or another, the concept has been with us for a very long time. Stretching back to ancient cultures, there is evidence of strong belief in the dead remaining with us in spirit. Folklore is full of stories about unexplained phenomena attributed to those unquiet spirits that are perhaps looking for revenge or longed-for but elusive rest, and many and varied are the rituals used to ensure that the spirits of the dead are at peace after their earthly trials.

The first ghost story recorded is attributed to the Roman playwright Plautus. Translated as *The Haunted House*, this work, unlike future scary tales, is a comedy and has no ghost! The haunting is an excuse to hide a son's misdemeanours from his father. Don't try this at home.

While in the earliest accounts ghosts were said to materialise as vapour, over time they came to be depicted as apparitions appearing as they would have looked at the time of their deaths. Hamlet's father, dressed in his full armour, and Banquo's ghost, appearing to Macbeth with his bloody wounds, are well-known examples.

It wasn't until the nineteenth century that the sheeted ghost that we know and love to dress up as makes a first appearance. And it was during the Victorian era that what we consider to be the classic ghost story came to the fore. A newly created middle class moved into houses that had servants, traditionally taken on at Michaelmas, when the nights were drawing in. New staff found themselves in an unknown house with its own peculiar creaks and groans. Servants were not expected to be seen or heard and many homes contained concealed doorways and corridors, meaning people would appear and disappear in front of others without warning. Lighting was often provided by gas lamps, the carbon monoxide they emitted provoking hallucinations. A breeding ground for ghostly tales!

One of the Victorian era's most celebrated novelists, Charles Dickens, of course gave us *A Christmas Carol*, with its ghost of Jacob Marley entwined by heavy chains – that idea itself wasn't new, though; the Ancient Roman writer Pliny the Younger's had written of a ghost bound in chains.

By the end of the Victorian era, M.R. James (1862-1936) had redefined the ghost story by abandoning many of the earlier gothic clichés and using more realistic settings. He wanted the reader to feel that what was in the story could happen to them.

Ghosts have far from faded from popular culture since then, whether on the page or screen. They have been depicted, by turns, as being romantic, scary, friendly, horrific and sometimes violent. Spirits involved can and do serve all manner of purposes. They appear as guardians of fate or seers with warnings of things yet to come. They can incite laughter or touch our conscience with their morality. They can inspire a shiver of fright, a frisson of despair or a quiet sigh of sorrow and loss.

And with interest in the paranormal far from being on the wane, we think the time is right for a collection in print of the best modern ghost stories – not a collection of old favourites or the usual suspects, not a collection of old ghost stories you might find elsewhere, but a collection of the best in new writing, the best in new short stories of the paranormal.

The genesis of this book has in part involved happy accident – and you can read a little bit more about that in Lewis Williams' introduction to *The Third Corona Book of Horror Stories*, published on the same day as this book. Suffice it to say here that this book is a project very close to our hearts and one that has been compiled from literally hundreds of short story submissions from across the globe.

Thanks go out to my co-conspirators who helped bring this book to print – I won't name you here, but you know who you are. We've tried to make this a book not just filled with great stories but with a varied selection of tales where the paranormal manifests itself in many and varied ways.

We've chosen to keep the stories in their respective authors' native version, or their choice of national version, of English; so you'll find some stories in American English or Canadian English rather than the whole book being presented uniformly in British English or American English. Depending on your point of view, we Brits will insist on adding 'u's to words where they're not needed, or Americans will keep missing out the letter 'u' from words like 'colour', and so on.

In keeping with presenting a truly modern collection of ghost stories, all of the stories have a contemporary (twenty-first century) setting.

We hope you enjoy reading *The Corona Book of Ghost Stories* and can help us make it the success the authors of these stories deserve.

Settle back and enjoy the ride. Our journey begins near a reservoir in Scotland …

Sue J. Eaton

DANGER: DEEP WATER

Jude Reid

I hate the reservoir, but then, I always did.

As long as I can remember there's been an iron fence around it, with an old yellow warning sign – 'Danger! Deaths have occurred at reservoirs' – but it was the picture that used to unsettle me the most. A black and white image, faded by time until it looked like a photocopy of a photocopy, an impressionist's sketch of a hand reaching out of the water, the body it belonged to totally submerged below. There was a story the big kids told that a boy had drowned here once, and I always thought of the hand as his. I dreamed of him for years, sunk to the bottom but still drifting upright, ankles tangled in pondweed and wire, hands forever straining towards the distant light of the surface.

When we got a bit older, we dared each other over the fence to throw stones into the water, poised for flight as if we were chucking bricks through a neighbour's window. The bravest would dip their toes in, then retreat, shrieking and giggling. Wee Calum MacLeod once waded out as far as the hems of his school shorts, securing the legendary status of hero and daredevil for the remainder of his time at junior school, before skill on the football pitch replaced raw courage as the primary determinant of social status.

The reservoir lost its hold on most of the kids over time, its dangerous allure replaced with the more reliable temptations of Buckfast, Silk Cut and sex. Not for me, though. It kept its place at the top of my list of terrors, a malevolent presence I had to pass at least twice a day on my journey to and from the school. Maybe it was coincidence, but I was half-convinced that Mhàiri Donnelly – five foot eight of nicotine-stained attitude with whom I had the misfortune to share a registration class – could sense how much I hated it, and deliberately chose the spot for my daily humiliations.

But it's not me in her sights today. Today it's someone else, and all I can feel is relief. The 'someone else' is the new girl, the only foreign kid in the school. I don't know her name. She sits in front of me in assembly, always with a headscarf tied round her hair, a different colour or pattern for every day of the week.

'Nobody wants you here,' Mhàiri Donnelly spits. She shoves the girl's shoulders, one hand on each side. 'You should fuck off back where you came from.'

The girl in the scarf stumbles and nearly falls, but despite the unbalancing weight of her schoolbag she keeps her footing and does the only thing possible, which is to keep walking through the mob and hope that eventually they get bored. I keep my distance, careful to avoid eye contact with anyone involved. I've been on the receiving end of Mhàiri often enough that I know how this goes. They'll keep worrying away at her like a pack of dogs until they get a reaction that justifies the kicking they've already decided to give her. Maybe they'll do it anyway.

There's sudden movement in the corner of my eye. I risk a glance and see Mhàiri grab the back of the girl's head and tug hard, earning herself a fistful of scarlet cloth.

'You want this back?' she says, waving it like a banner. 'Come on and get it then.'

The girl keeps her head down.

'What are you going to do if the boys see your hair?' Mhàiri's voice is full of mock concern, accompanied by an obedient titter from her sidekicks. With a gust of wind, the scarf billows like a sail. Mhàiri grins and opens her hand. 'Whoops.'

The headscarf rises, dancing like a flame over the fence, to hang reflected in the stillness of the reservoir; then it drops like a diving bird, to land and congeal on the water's surface. Mhàiri and her mob erupt in laughter; then, satisfied for now, they weave off towards the village green, voices ringing with mockery as they go.

When I look back, the girl's staring at me, the wariness in her expression making it clear she's wondering if I'm another one of her tormentors.

'I'm not with them,' I say hastily. 'In fact, most days it's me they're messing with. I'm sorry they've started on you.'

'It's all right,' she says with a shrug. 'What do they pick on you for, then?'

I slide out from under the question. 'You know what they're like, any excuse. It's mostly 'cos I won't lick Mhàiri's arse like the rest of them.'

That gets a smile. 'I'm Safiya.'

'Kerry. D'you want my scarf? For, you know—' I wave my hand in a vague halo around my face.

'No thanks.' She shakes her head. 'It's no big deal. I don't wear one all the time anyway.'

'I'd be raging if it was me. And it usually is me. Not the headscarf thing, I mean, but they've chucked my bag in a couple of times and my jacket once. It sank. I had to tell my dad I lost it, and he was raging for weeks. Bunch of arseholes.'

'Arseholes,' she echoes. The word sounds wrong in her almost-American accent.

'Total arseholes,' I agree. 'You're from Syria, yeah?'

She nods. It's not a secret. The news made the papers when her family were rehomed here, reported as some sort of miracle of multicultural acceptance – 'Rural community takes refugees to its heart' – although what I'd heard the locals saying off the record wasn't suitable for publication. In the village – population seven hundred and eight – new faces stick out like the proverbial sore thumb, especially if they're a different colour from the usual.

'You speak really good English.'

Another shrug. 'We did it at school. And we watched a lot of American TV.'

She slings her schoolbag over the fence, and climbs after it to sit on the cobbles at the water's edge. I follow her, feeling a familiar transgressive thrill at the reservoir's proximity.

'Do you not need to be getting home?' I ask.

'No. Mom's on late shift at the Co-op, and Adnan doesn't get out of after school club until five. I've got to pick him up then.'

'Adnan's your brother?'

She nods. 'He's at the primary school. He likes his teacher. He says the other kids are nice.' Her mouth twists, maybe with envy. 'I have to take him home a different way. He won't go past the water. Apparently there's something in it.'

She's speaking sarcastically, of course, but a prickle of fear runs over my skin. I try and hide my unease with a laugh.

'I think every kid in the village goes through that phase. He's maybe just picked it up from someone at the school.'

'Mom says it's probably because of the boat we had to go on, when we left home. We were on it for ages. It got really bad for a while.' She doesn't offer up any more detail, and I don't want to ask – not now anyway. 'It's not a big surprise he doesn't like water anymore. It is pretty creepy here, though.'

The thin winter sunlight is starting to fade as the wind picks up, sending ripples across the reservoir's surface. I think of murky green depths, and clawed hands, fish-belly white.

'Yeah, it is a bit.' But creepy or not, it's nice sitting with her. I find myself wondering if she'd like to be friends, and stifle the nursery school urge to ask her to my house for tea. She's in the third year, I remind myself, and maybe she doesn't want to hang out with some eedjit from the year below.

And then everything goes wrong again.

'They're coming back.'

She follows my gaze, and her face falls as she sees Mhàiri and her chief sycophant returning, clearly intent on finishing what they'd started.

'Aw, did you not get your scarf, then?' Mhàiri says, voice dripping with mock sympathy.

'Fuck off, Mhàiri,' I say, suddenly bold, and give her the finger.

'What did you just say?'

Some of the shock on her face is feigned for effect, but most of it seems to be genuine astonishment. She turns to her lackey. 'Did you hear her tell me to fuck off?'

Mhàiri dumps her school bag and heads straight over the fence towards us at terrifying speed. I've only got a second to regret my bravado before her hands grab my blazer and drag me to my feet. 'You don't get to talk to me like that, you cheeky wee shite.'

I try to step back, but my ankle catches on something – the strap of my rucksack, I realise – and I lose my footing entirely, slipping backwards down the slick cobbles. The sudden shift in weight takes Mhàiri off guard, but she's too intent on giving me a beating to let go in time, and the next moment the pair of us are falling towards the black mirror of the reservoir.

The surface shatters around us, and the chill beneath takes my breath away. I struggle up, scrabbling blindly at Mhàiri's shoulders and head, sucking air with desperate lungs that seem to have forgotten how to work. Mhàiri breaches beside me like a furious whale, crimson with fury and humiliation. She snarls, a raw animal sound, reaching out to shove me back under the water.

Something locks around my wrist, and I scream out what little air I have left – but it's Safiya who's waded out waist deep in the water to grab me, and who's now doing her best to pull me ashore.

It seems Mhàiri has other plans. She's found her footing, and she uses the extra stability to grab my head and push it down hard. It's almost unbelievable. Mhàiri's a terror, a bully, but surely she's not meaning to drown me? My limbs churn uselessly at the surface – I realise that somehow I've managed to twist free of Safiya's grip, and I'm wholly at Mhàiri's mercy, the world around me turning cloudy with bubbles.

And that's when it happens. Without the use of any sense I can name, I become aware of something with us in the water, rising out of the black depths with tangible intent. It's the feeling I've had in nightmares but never experienced awake – an appalling sort of sick dread, the kind that comes when your legs won't carry you away from whatever horror's pursuing you across your subconscious – except this isn't a dream. I'm wide awake, I'm drowning, and I can't make my feet find purchase on the mould-slick concrete slope. Mhàiri can sense it too, I can tell – she's still pushing at me, but now I'm just another object she can use to push herself towards dry land and safety. Safiya's shouting, stretching out for me with one hand and Mhàiri with the other, all lesser enmities forgotten, and with her help I finally heave myself out of the reservoir onto the wet cobbles. The water churns in my wake, and I turn to see Mhàiri still waist deep, locked hand-to-wrist with Safiya, making no progress in spite of their combined efforts. I reach for her other hand and pull, but she's stuck fast, breathless and gasping, eyes bulging with panic.

'Come on!' I scream, and we heave in desperation, our combined force just enough to pull Mhàiri halfway up the ground beside us.

As her foot breaks the surface, I see it. A hand, or the remains of one, the flesh bloated and grey with long submersion. The nails are cracked, yellow talons – the fingers are locked around Mhàiri's ankle tight enough to blanch and bruise her skin. As she kicks and strains to break its hold, I catch a glimpse of a bone-grey wrist, a filthy rag that once might have been a shirt cuff or a shroud – and the shadow below it, rising to the surface, coalescing like a pool of oil.

Mhàiri lashes out with her other heel, and the strength of her desperation is enough to break the hand's grip. The yellow nails rip furrows down her skin as she hauls herself free and scrabbles for dry land. The hand closes on empty air, opens again, and then, without warning, it slides silently down. The shadow beneath the surface widens and blurs, until it, too, is indistinguishable from the water around it.

'Did that just…' Mhàiri begins, then lapses back into silence.

The three of us sit in silence, leaning into the fence and each other, as the lead-grey water darkens to black, and the red chiffon scarf drifts across its surface like a bloodstain.

LIGEIA

Mike Sherer

The last thing Michael expected to see when he arrived that first morning to work on the old house he had just purchased was someone inside it. The house had been unoccupied for decades. Yet as he drove nearer up the long dirt lane he saw a woman standing in an upstairs window.

The room she was in sat atop a four-story tower. It looked like an enclosed widow's walk, with a pair of floor-to-ceiling windows in each of its four walls. Along with the bay windows and profusion of intricate gingerbread wood trim, the house was an architectural oddity for Kansas. That's what had attracted Michael to it. Kansas people were too practical for such frippery; they preferred spare solid houses that could withstand the tornados that passed by with regularity.

Michael looked up as he climbed out of his pickup. She was unmoved, still staring into the sun. As he waded through knee-high grass his main concern was for the woman, not his house. It wasn't safe to climb so high on those old stairs. He had inspected the house, of course, before buying it. It had good bones. The roof was mostly intact. The foundation was solid. The wood shutters had protected most of the glass. But over a century of weather and settling had weakened the walls and warped the floors and damaged many other parts of the construction.

None of these defects were serious enough to deter Michael. The house was a historical gem. He realized a large investment of money and labor was required to make it livable and update it for the twenty-first century. But this was a worthwhile endeavor for him. He had a passion for bringing such forlorn buildings back to life, especially one as structurally unique as this.

Even with his light tread, the aged wood bowed and groaned under his feet as he mounted the steps and crossed the porch. Michael was a small slight man, which had always been a boon for him in both his current profession and his previous one. He could easily maneuver around and slip into and out of the tight interiors where he had always labored.

Michael opened the front door, left unlocked because he would rather people walk in than break in. So the woman hadn't actually broken into his house. More than likely she hadn't vandalized anything, either. Perhaps she was homeless and was seeking shelter.

The early morning light through the filthy windows only dimly lit the front room Michael entered. He strode through shadows of suspended dust, across the slanted floor to the stairs. Having been up these steps several times already, he knew where to place his foot on each to produce the least creak. The woman surely had seen him arrive, but there was no need to further announce his presence in a threatening way.

On the second floor there was even more dust hanging in the airless air. So much that, upon glancing through an open door into a barren room, the motes seemed to coalesce into the shape of a small boy playing on the floor. Michael blinked, and the form dissipated. He leaned in to look around. Could this have been a child's bedroom? Nothing remained to suggest what use the space had been put to.

Michael continued through the smudged sunlight up to the third floor. He crossed directly to the staircase, steep and narrow with no railing, that led on up to the room where he had seen the woman. Climbing these stairs was like emerging from a basement into the outdoors. The space was brilliantly lit by the morning sun. Each of the four walls consisted of more glass than wood, giving an astounding view in all directions.

In this dazzling light he saw the woman had not moved; she was still standing stiffly erect gazing out to the east. He could not conceive of her being homeless. Her voluminous white gown that hung down to her bare feet was spotless. Her long black hair that spilled down over bare shoulders without twist or knot glowed like polished onyx. Those bare feet and shoulders and all other exposed skin was without grime or blemish. Homeless? No way. Then what?

She was so still Michael considered she might not be real. Could she be a mannequin? Could someone have brought it up here as a joke? He sucked in a lungful of stale air, then released it in a single tentative word, "Miss?"

She turned to face him.

Bang! Michael jumped so he nearly fell down the steps. Bang! It came from below. Bang! He stared down into the shadows of the third floor. Bang! He looked back to the woman. She was gone. Bright morning sunlight illuminated an empty space. Bang!

Now Michael was so rattled by the sudden racket and so confused by the woman's sudden disappearance that he did lose his footing. He tumbled down the steep stairs. Sprawled at the foot of them, he felt so weak and light-headed he could hardly move. Had he hit his head? He felt but could find no bump or blood. What had happened to him? Why did he feel so weak? He poked around other parts of his body but could locate no serious pain. Bang! He had to get up and go see what that noise was. It was coming from below; he must go down.

Carefully, slowly, Michael regained his footing and cautiously approached the next flight of stairs. He was weak and dizzy, on the verge of passing out. Had something in the house affected him? He had been all through the house several times, and there had been no injurious reaction to the stale air or all the accumulated crud. Holding securely onto the rail, he limped down to the second floor, then on down to the first. He could hardly plant one foot below the other; only by clinging to the railing did he keep from collapsing.

Bang! Reaching the bottom floor, Michael realized the racket was coming from someone pounding on the front door. He tried to yell at whoever it was to stop, he was coming, but it only came out as a croak. What was wrong with him? He could hardly make a sound. He staggered across the front room and opened the door, leaning on it heavily for support.

A middle-aged man stood on the front porch, his right fist poised to whack the door again. It was the contractor, Gerald, hired to help rehab the old house. "Why are you beating down the door?" Michael wheezed.

"I saw you upstairs," Gerald replied, frowning, "through the windows. In that top room."

Michael clung to the open door to keep from pitching over. "So? It's my house."

"That I'm supposed to be working on."

"Why didn't you just come in. It wasn't locked," Michael panted, gasping for air, gulping for moisture to speak with.

"Are you okay?"

"I was. Until you started trying to beat my front door down."

"You look bad. And that scroungy beard doesn't help."

"I don't have a beard." Michael felt his chin. There was several days growth.

"When's the last time you took a shower? Or changed clothes?" Gerald sniffed, then grinned. "Have you peed your pants?"

Michael looked down at himself. His work clothes were covered with grime like he had been wallowing around the filthy floor of the house. And the front of his pants was damp. He sagged against the door frame.

Gerald reached out to catch him, then thought better of touching him and stepped back. "Are you sick?"

"No. I just feel weak."

"Come on, I'll drive you back to town."

"I've got my truck."

"Yeah, but you don't need to be driving, shape you're in." Gerald gave a lopsided grin. "I hope you can walk. I really don't want to carry you, way you are."

"There's a woman upstairs. In that tower room you saw me in. She was standing in the window. You must have seen her."

Gerald shook his head. "All I saw was you."

"I need to find out why she's here." Michael pushed off from the door frame and took two staggering steps.

"Hold on," Gerald said, coming up from behind. "You can't even walk across the room. You won't make it up three flights of stairs. I'll find out what's going on."

Michael nodded, retreating back to the door frame while Gerald went up the stairs.

Several minutes later Gerald returned. Alone. "Where is she?" Michael asked.

Gerald shook his head. "There's nobody here but us."

"Bullshit. I saw her. She looked at me. Did you search all the rooms?"

"I did. No one's here." He stepped up to Michael. "You're seeing things, Mike. The shape you're in, that's no surprise." Michael limped out across the porch and hobbled down the steps. Gerald followed him closely across the front lawn toward his truck, ready to catch him if necessary. "Let me get some plastic for you to sit on."

"Why don't I just climb in the bed."

"Not a bad idea."

Michael stopped at the passenger door to glare at Gerald. "I can hire another contractor. One without such a smart mouth."

"You better be able to, because this one almost quit on

you. We were supposed to get started on this place three days ago."

"Bullshit."

"I've been waiting for you to call. You wouldn't answer my calls. So I finally came out here to see what was going on."

"Three days? I got here ten minutes ago."

"Look at yourself, Mike." Michael gazed into the side view mirror on Gerald's pickup. He looked like crap. Unshaven filthy crap. "Does that look like ten minutes?" Michael was frozen, staring at his reflection. Three days? It couldn't be. But it sure looked like it. And felt like it. He was faint with hunger, and his throat was so dry he could hardly talk. "I was kidding about the plastic. Just get in." Michael opened the door and hauled himself up into the seat. "The seat's got good stain guard." Gerald smiled, lowering both windows. "Whoo-wee. We do need to get some fresh air in here."

As Gerald turned around, making a wide circle in the front yard, Michael looked up to the top tower room. The window the young woman had been at was empty. Where in the hell had she gone? Gerald completed the circle and drove away down the long lane.

Three days. Michael couldn't get over it. Where had three days gone? He couldn't dispute Gerald. There was the length of his beard, the condition of his clothes, the condition he was in… When Gerald dropped him off at his long-term motel room he ate and drank just enough to keep any more damage from happening, then shaved and showered, then collapsed into a clean bed for twelve hours. When he awoke he dressed in gloriously clean clothes and feasted at a nearby breakfast buffet. Then he waddled back to his room and slept eight more hours. When he awoke late that afternoon he felt rested. Physically.

Mentally, he was a mess. Three days had disappeared from his life. Had he blacked out? Apparently. But why? He wasn't a heavy drinker. He didn't use illegal drugs. He wasn't on any strong prescription medication. Had he had a stroke? Maybe. He needed to see a doctor. But he also needed to work on that house. It was costing him money every day it sat there with him doing no work on it, and three days had already slipped by. He needed to get this rehab done and sell it. Then he would see a doctor. Maybe it was a quirk, a one-time incident. But what would have happened to him if Gerald hadn't shown up? Would he have wasted away in that house? Could he have died? So he wouldn't go there again without Gerald. And he would keep a close watch on himself. And he definitely wouldn't chase after any more intruders.

Yet Michael couldn't stop thinking about her. He had heard tales about the house. He had done his due diligence before buying it. The people in the small farming community had been eager to relate their ghost stories – which he had ignored, not being in the least superstitious. But now that he had seen, what, a ghost? he still couldn't bring himself to acknowledge such a thing. His brain had suffered some kind of mishap. If he could lose three days, he could easily hallucinate. Yet he couldn't stop dwelling upon the woman he had seen. She was beautiful. And he hadn't felt threatened at all. If she actually was a spirit, she seemed a benign one.

That evening Michael went out for another hearty meal. After, he walked to a small local tavern to make some discrete inquiries. He found one old codger whose tongue loosened considerably with each drink Michael bought him. "You know why that damned house looks like it does?"

"Because it's sat empty for years," Michael answered.

"I'm not talking about the way it looks. I'm talking about the way it was built."

"It is an unusual design. That's what attracted me to it."

"It wouldn't be unusual for other parts of the country. But here in Kansas, what's the point of it? That lookout? To see what? Acres of wheat?"

"It reminds me of a widow's walk, enclosed and with a roof."

"That's exactly what it is. I seen pictures of them, on tops of houses in New England. In earlier days fishing and whaling trips were long and dangerous. Sailors' wives watched for their husbands' safe return from those perches on top their houses. Many didn't return. That's how they got the name widow's walk. The man who built the house, Cal Walker, came here from Massachusetts. He'd sailed on whaling ships and fishing ships most his life. Then he decided he wanted to do something different."

"I can relate to that," Michael interjected.

"Or he saw something out at sea that spooked him. Spooked him so bad he got two thousand miles away from that sea."

"What did he see?"

"Never said. But all them miles didn't distance him from trouble. What did he expect, coming here with such a young good-looking wife?"

Michael drew erect at this. "What did she look like?"

"Never saw her myself. Before my time. And there weren't no pictures. It's just said she was a black-haired beauty."

"What kind of trouble happened?"

"I'm getting to it." The old man indiscreetly coughed. "My throat's getting dry from all this talking. It's not used to so many words passing through it."

Michael doubted that last statement yet ordered another beer for his companion. "I assume he designed his house to be similar to what he was used to seeing on the Massachusetts coast."

"Could be," the old man said after downing half of his fresh mug of beer. "Could be he was keeping a watch for something coming after him."

"A sea creature? Coming to Kansas?"

"I never claimed it was a sea monster what spooked him. No one knows what it was spooked him."

"Whatever it was, it got him?"

"Nothing got him. He killed himself. Blew his brains out."

"What happened to his wife?"

"He killed her. And their little boy. And the man she was fooling around with. *Then* he killed himself."

"That's terrible."

"It is. Near as terrible as the other two times it happened."

Michael, perched on the edge of his seat, stared across the table at the old man, who merely rattled his empty mug on the tabletop. Michael ordered it to be refilled.

Once it was, the old man continued, "First time, a man and his sister went in together on it. He was a bachelor, while she was a widow with two children. The brother killed her and both her children, then killed himself. Second time, a single man bought the place. Found him dead by his own hand, too. No one's touched the place since." The old man leaned back in his chair with a smile. "Until you."

Michael was on edge the following morning as Gerald turned in the lane leading to the house. He gazed up at the windows of the top tower room. She wasn't there. After Gerald parked, Michael got out to look over his pickup. It appeared undisturbed. "Didn't think anyone would bother it," Gerald said. "Everyone around here thinks this place is haunted. Won't come near it." Michael merely nodded as he unlocked his toolboxes, while Gerald continued, "Hope you aren't expecting me to work out here three days straight like you did. I've got a wife and family to go home to at night."

As the pair walked up onto the porch, Michael saw that the front door was ajar. He glared at Gerald. "Didn't you close it good?"

"Sure did. Maybe a ghost opened it?" Gerald laughed. "You've been listening to old Cory down at the Pleasure Inn. I heard you were in there last night asking questions. Tales travel fast in this little town. Maybe someone overheard you and Cory and got interested enough in this place to come out here to see what you're doing."

As they walked in Gerald looked around, shaking his head. "Damn, Mike, you sure didn't get much done for being here three days."

They worked in the basement. It was dark and cool and clammy, with a deep musty smell hanging densely over a hard-packed dirt floor. The low-ceiling room was empty, except for the impressive spider webs strung everywhere. Several of the support beams needed to be replaced. Michael and Gerald got busy bracing the first-story floor so they could cut out and replace the rotten wood.

Michael had not been laboring in the basement long when he noticed something on a wall. Picking up his flashlight, he saw letters had been scratched into the old blocks. Ligeia. "Gerald, come look at this." Gerald joined him. "What do you think it means?"

"Looks like graffiti. Kids been down here."

"This place? With all the stories? I don't think so. Besides, it doesn't look like English. Latin, maybe?"

"Who cares? Just sandpaper it off."

"No. It adds character. If the new owners don't like it, they can remove it."

Later that day when Michael went upstairs for some tools he saw a young boy, about five or so, playing on the floor in the doorway leading into the kitchen. His old-fashioned clothes seemed clean for him to be sitting on such a dirty floor. He looked up at Michael and smiled, then stood and walked into the kitchen. Michael followed him. The room was empty, but the back door was open. Michael went to the back door to look out. The boy was nowhere in sight, but large nets were spread out all across the backyard. A crooked old man was bent over working on them. "Who are you?"

The old man looked up from the nets. His weathered face had an unkempt gray beard, while gray hair spilled out from under a cap. His ragged patched clothes seemed heavy, especially the coat, for such a warm clime. When he smiled there were more gaps than teeth in his rotted gums. He straightened as far as his bent back would allow, drawing out a wicked long blade as he did.

Michael stepped back. Into Gerald's arms. Michael jerked away in fear, while Gerald sighed, frowning. "What's going on now?"

Michael looked out to the backyard. It was empty. No old man brandishing a knife, no nets spread out on the ground, no young boy. Nothing but high grass and several falling-down outbuildings. He turned back to confront the scowl. "Nothing."

Gerald leaned around him to look out into the back yard. "What's out there?"

"If I told you, you wouldn't believe me."

Gerald stepped back. "Try me."

"An old fisherman mending his nets."

"Fishing nets. In the middle of Kansas." Gerald took another step back, with a deep sigh. "So Cory tells you the story last night about the old guy who built this place, and now you see him. Awfully convenient."

"You asked."

"You came up to get some tools." Michael nodded, then started back across the kitchen. Gerald blocked his path. "A half-hour ago."

"No way."

Gerald raised his phone with the time displayed up to Michael's face. "More like forty minutes." He lowered the phone. "You need to find another contractor."

"Really?"

"I'll help you finish bracing the floor. I know that's a two-man job, and I won't leave you in the lurch. But after that I'm done. I wasn't crazy about working on this old house to begin with. Way you're behaving, now I don't want anything to do with it. Think we can finish in the basement without you zoning out again?"

Michael and Gerald worked until late in the afternoon. When they came upstairs it was well past dinner time. "Another day and we'll be done in the basement," Michael said. "Will you come back to finish tomorrow?"

"I told you I'll work until we're done in the basement."

"Good." Michael dug a key out of his pocket and handed it to him. "Front door key. In case it's locked when you come tomorrow."

Gerald pocketed the key. "What time will you get here?"

"I'm not leaving. I'm spending the night." Gerald looked at him as if he were unhinged. "Something's going on here. I want to find out what."

Gerald grinned. "Should I bring the coroner with me in the morning?"

"Just be sure to come. I don't want to lose another three days."

Gerald walked out shaking his head, leaving Michael standing in the open front door watching Gerald's pickup disappear down the long lane.

Michael descended back into the basement to accomplish all he could on his own while he still had good light. He wasn't frightened. His encounters with the three ghosts, for he believed that's what they were despite his lifelong skepticism, had not been frightening. Even the old man with the knife. Michael realized he had been using it to work on his fishing nets; he hadn't threatened Michael with it. Michael hadn't felt threatened by any of the ghosts. And Gerald would check on him in the morning, so he wouldn't die of thirst like he nearly had several days ago.

When Michael came up from the basement in the dusky light the woman was awaiting him. She appeared same as before, in her long white gown, standing barefoot in the middle of the front room. "Who are you?"

She turned and walked to the stairs. Something slithered across the floor in a dark corner. The woman's eyes flashed. "Luke!" The creature darted across the floor along the wall and out into the hall.

"What was that?"

She smiled without replying and ascended the stairs, loosening her gown as she went. Michael was rooted to the foot of the stairs as the luminous material slid down from her ivory shoulders. At the top step she let the gown cascade down her perfect skin to the floor. Michael only glimpsed her beauty before she disappeared into a room, but the image was seared into the backs of his eyes. Michael dropped his toolbox and hastily followed up the stairs.

"What the hell?" Michael opened his eyes, then squinched them nearly shut again. It was bright daylight. Sunlight flooded the tower room. He located Gerald standing in the open doorway, snickering. It was then he realized he was lying naked on the floor. Gerald turned away. "I won't ask. Just come on down to the basement when you get your clothes on. I want to finish down there and get the hell away from this place." Gerald started down the steep stairs, calling back, "By the way, nice tat."

Michael glanced at the tattoo on his right shoulder, an anchor with 'U.S. NAVY' and 'Silent Service' emblazoned above and below it. Then he closed his eyes and strained his memory. Nothing came. The woman had disrobed at the top of the stairs. He'd gotten a good look at her naked beauty. Then? She'd walked away out of sight. And? He had followed her up the stairs. And? Nothing. Michael couldn't remember being with her. He couldn't even remember reaching the top of the stairs. Damn! What had happened?

He felt his privates. He was sticky. Could he have had a wet dream? Or had he masturbated? He raised his fingertips to his nose. Was there a different scent? From another body? Her body? He couldn't tell. Damn, why couldn't he remember?

He suddenly remembered. He had seen some creature. She had called it Luke. Was it her son? But it hadn't looked like the little boy he'd seen earlier. This thing was beastly. Maybe she had two children, and this one was deformed. But it was more than deformed. It was monstrous.

"Hey, Mike!" Gerald called out from below. "You dressed yet? Let's get going! You and this place are creeping me out!"

With a groan, Michael stirred. He felt worn out, like he had been awake all night. Like he had been making love all night? He gingerly touched his shriveled sticky member. Somebody had abused him last night, a ghost, or his right hand? Sitting upright, he located his clothes tossed in a corner. He hoisted himself up and looked himself over. He was covered with filth like he had been rolling on the floor. He stumbled over to his clothes and staggered into them.

They finished working in the basement by early afternoon. Michael helped Gerald gather up his tools and carry them out to his truck. After they were put away, Gerald turned to Michael with an apologetic wince. "Will you be all right?"

Michael smiled. "Sure. I'm glad you stuck around to help me finish in the basement." Gerald hung his head. "I'm lucky I got anyone to come work on this place, with the reputation it has."

Gerald looked up at that. "This place doesn't bother me. It's you."

Michael shrugged. "I don't know what's going on."

"I'll check on you. Don't want you killing yourself." Realizing what he had just said, Gerald hastily continued, "I mean by starving to death. I didn't mean by blowing your brains out."

"Like the other lunatics did," Michael finished the thought for him. "I appreciate it." Gerald offered the door key back, but Michael declined to take it. "Keep it. If you're coming out to check on me sometime."

Gerald nodded, slipping the key back into his pocket. "How long were you in the Navy?"

"Ten years."

"Where'd you serve?"

"On a submarine. The Jacksonville, Los Angeles Attack Class, based in Pearl Harbor."

"Hawaii. Not a bad assignment. Why'd you get out?"

"I wanted to do something else."

Gerald chuckled. "This is as something else as it gets, in the smack middle of the continent." Gerald climbed in his pickup and drove away.

After watching him drive away down the lane, Michael walked up to the front porch – to find the five-year-old boy playing with a wooden sailboat. "Do you have a brother?" he asked. The boy looked up at him, smiled, shook his head no, then busied himself with his toy once again. "Is your name Luke?"

"Leukon," the boy answered, without looking up from his toy boat.

Michael started to go back into the house but stopped halfway through the door when a sudden movement in the corner of his eye arrested him. The thing he had seen the night before, that had slithered across the floor into a room, it had just slithered from where the boy had been, off the porch into the yard. Michael leaned over the porch rail to look. It was gone. But the sailboat remained. Michael picked it up. It was rough-made, as if it had been whittled out of a block of wood. Its only decoration was a trident carved into the side.

Later that afternoon Michael was ripping out some ruined plaster in the front room on the first floor when he discovered a large piece of wood concealed inside the wall. He broke more plaster away to free it. It was an irregular section of planking, weathered and bereft of paint, that appeared to have been broken off rather than sawed. Pulling it out, he saw something had been inscribed. Ligeia. The same word he had seen on the basement wall.

Michael sniffed. A new scent was in the air. Not the smell of sun-ripened wheat from outside or the usual musty aged smell from inside. Salt. Fish. The sea. Michael followed his nose in a searching circuit of the room, until he spied the old man he had seen in the back yard tending to fishing nets. He was standing in a corner, half concealed in shadows. "That be off my old fishing boat. Wanted to bring a bit of sea with me to this dry place."

Michael stepped back toward the front door. "Are you angry with me?"

The old man gummed a nearly-toothless grin. "Yea."

"I'm sorry. I've seen your wife, but I don't remember doing anything to her."

The old man cackled. "Ain't that a pisser? What good is sinning if you don't have the joy of remembering it?"

"Are you going to hurt me?"

"Why do you reckon I would do that? You're a man of the sea, like me. Hard to come by in this part of the country."

"Everyone who ever lived in your house died. Violently."

"Murder, suicide, yea, there be some crazy people lived here."

"I'm not crazy."

"My wife tends to drive men crazy."

"I'm sorry. For whatever I did."

"Not entirely your fault. She's got a mighty sweet song." The old man turned and disappeared into the shadows.

That night as dusk settled Michael went out to his pickup for his sleeping bag and his pistol, a SIG P228 M11. It was the same model he was issued in the Navy, one he had been well-trained on and felt comfortable using. Closing the door, he instinctively looked up to the top tower room. There she stood as the first time he had seen her, in her white gown standing before a window in the covered widow's walk gazing his way. This time Michael realized she wasn't looking at him; she was looking far beyond him to the eastern horizon. He considered his options. He could go to her, as he had done twice before. Or he could get in his truck and drive away, never to return. He had already put most of his tools away; the few still in the house could easily be replaced. He would take a big hit on the house, of course, but it wouldn't bankrupt him; he would survive. He did not doubt what the old salt had said, that he was going crazy. That she was driving him crazy. He should just drive off and never look back.

Then he heard it. Her song. It floated down from on high. The night sharpened with its melody. The stars, every star in the sky, blossomed into Bethlehem's Star, each one marking this miracle. The shadows shifted into magical forms, sliding and darting and twisting through the dark. The blades of grass sparkled like a host of fairies, each blade a pinhead upon which an infinity of angels danced.

And the house. It changed. Without a sound the boards stretched, bending into a new shape. A sailing ship, with the old sailor on what had been the front porch but was now the prow, and the young boy sitting on what had been the ledge of an open second-floor window but was now a railing on an upper deck, and the beautiful singer in what had been the top tower room but was now the crow's nest. Michael panicked. The ship was sailing off into the night without him. He ran to the front porch with his sleeping bag and jumped.

The old sailor caught his arm and pulled him on board. "It's a marvelous night to be sailing the wheat."

Michael looked all around. The boat was slicing through the golden waves. Then he looked to the old man. "You helped me. Pulled me on board. You want me here. Why?"

"She's taking on water. You've seen the shape she's in. She needs to be dry docked. You got a lot of work to do to make her seaworthy again. I don't want her sailing the way you're used to sailing, under the waves. Though that must be a wondrous thing." The old man turned away to gaze out to the field they were sailing. "That be tomorrow. Tonight, enjoy her song."

Michael stepped up to the porch rail alongside the old sailor, closed his eyes, and listened with all his soul to the music of the spheres resonating through the marrow of his bones.

"Hey! Mike! Are you decent?!"

Michael opened his eyes. He wasn't. But at least he wasn't so filthy this morning. He had awakened in his sleeping bag instead of on the bare floor.

"Come on, Mike! Answer me! I don't want to have to come up there and see what I saw yesterday!"

"I'm okay, Gerald! I be right down!" Michael looked around. He found his clothes in the same corner of the top tower room as before, only this time neatly folded. He climbed naked from his bag to get dressed.

Michael joined Gerald on the front porch. "You okay?" Gerald asked.

Michael smiled. "I be fine."

"You look better than you did yesterday morning. Especially with your clothes on. Here." Gerald offered a thermos of coffee and a bag of doughnuts.

"Thank ye, Gerald."

Gerald stared as Michael poured a cup. "Why are you talking like that?" Michael looked up at him with an inquisitive gaze. "Like a cartoon pirate."

Michael laughed. "Sorry." He took a deep gulp. "Aye, this be fine. Uhh, this is good."

"Don't expect it every morning. I just wanted to make sure you were okay."

"To see if I'd blown my brains out yet?"

"Yeah."

"No, I'm good. I'm better than good. I've got my sea legs back."

"In Kansas."

"I never realized how much I missed the sea."

"Have you seen any more ghosts?"

"Yes, three of them."

"And you're okay with that?"

"They're not going to hurt me. They need me."

After that morning, Michael gave up his motel room and moved into the house. He was still seen around town – at the hardware store, the lumber yard, restaurants, the Pleasure Inn. Most people kept their distance, especially once any of them got close enough to see the extent of his deterioration. He was a small man to begin with, but he soon was whittled down to a nib. While his frame shrank, his wild hair grew, entangling with the barbarous sprays and kinks of wiry gray hair that burst from his wizened face. His eyes sank; his soul seemed to shrivel. He was worn down to much less than what he had been.

It became difficult for him to get the lumber yard to make deliveries. No one wanted to drive out to the haunted house and deal with the crazy man. But each time it did happen the delivery driver returned to the yard with amazing stories of the transformation taking place. They said Michael must be working around the clock to get so much done by himself. Naturally, some of the townspeople asserted that he couldn't do so much by himself, that he was getting some ungodly help. That assertion seemed supported by his exhausted and ever-worsening condition. As the house waxed, Michael waned. As time went by, he made fewer and fewer appearances in town.

On his penultimate trip into town Michael ventured late one night into the Pleasure Inn. This time Cory bought Michael drinks. "You sure looked peaked," the old man said. "I hear you're working yourself to death."

Michael grinned, presenting a rictal gash. "Ain't the work wearing me out."

"Don't know why you're in such a hurry. Nobody's going to buy that place, even if you get it to looking brand spanking new."

"Don't know if I want to sell it, now."

"You going to live in it?"

"Or sail away in it."

Michael's final trip into town was to the library. His appearance so disturbed the librarian she immediately approached him. "Can I help you?"

"Ligeia." She waited, at a safe distance, for more information. He gave it. "L-i-g-e-i-a. Ligeia. Do you know it?"

"Is it the name of a book you are looking for?" He scowled at her. "We can google it." She led the way to a computer and entered the name in the search engine. "Ligeia," she read, surprised at having found it. "It's a short story by Edgar Allan Poe." She looked up. "We have several good collections of Poe stories."

"It's not a book. It's a boat."

"I suppose there could be a boat named that." The librarian returned her attention to the computer screen. She scrolled to the very bottom of the page. "Ligeia meaning. Let's see where that takes us." She clicked on the link. "Ligeia. Clear-voiced. The name of one of the Sirens from Greek mythology."

Michael smiled in such a way the librarian paled. "Yea. Ev'ry sailor knows the Sirens. They beguile seamen with their singing to wreck upon the rocks. That be her." Michael brusquely walked out, leaving the librarian staring after him.

That night Michael stood on the front porch beside the old sailor, staring out at the waves of wheat. "Is Ligeia your wife's name?"

"You been bedding her without even asking her name?"

"I have no recollection of being in bed with her."

"Your recollecting seems faulty."

"Why did you move here?"

"Had to get as far away from the sea as I could."

"Why?"

"Got me one hell of a father-in-law." Michael burst out laughing, and the old man joined in.

One day Michael was working in a third-floor room when he heard someone moving about above him. He climbed the steep stairs and looked in. The woman stood in her customary position in her white gown, gazing out upon the front yard. She didn't acknowledge Michael as he climbed the rest of the way up. "Why do you stay up here?" She never diverted her eyes. "Are you watching for your father? Is Poseidon coming to take you back to the sea?" The woman turned to him with a trace of a smile.

"Why did you come here, Ligeia? With your husband? If you hate it so badly?"

The smile transformed into a frightening visage. "That maggot is not my husband! He caught me in his foul nets, dragged me so far from the sea I could never get back." She returned her stare outside. "On my own."

Late one afternoon Michael gathered his tools up from the third-floor room he was working in. It was growing dark, and he was careless with fatigue and anticipation of the night's pleasures. At the top of the stairs, he tripped. He flung his tools away as he pitched forward, then grabbed at the banister as he tumbled. Half-way down the stairs he broke his fall. Looking back up, he saw the dark form the woman called Luke slither away from the top of the stairs into a third-floor room. Was that what he had tripped on? Had that monster tripped him on purpose? Michael arched his back, stretched his neck, and poked around his body to determine if anything was broken. He seemed intact. Slowly, he stood and limped down to the second floor, gathering his tools as he went.

Late one evening Michael placed the board that had come from Cal Walker's old ship, which was inscribed with the name Ligeia, upon the wooden mantle above the brick fireplace. Smelling the open sea once again, he looked over his shoulder to find the old sailor in a shadowy corner nodding approvingly. "Her son tried to kill me."

"That be my boy, too."

"That thing?"

"He's a half-breed. Sometimes he looks like hers. Sometimes he looks like mine."

"Sometimes he looks like a monster."

"On land. In water he looks quite elegant."

"Why does he want to hurt me?"

"You're spending too much time with his mother. He don't like that." The old man grinned. "I don't like it neither."

"But you need me." The old sailor nodded. "To make repairs on your ship." The old man nodded still. "What happens when the repairs are done?"

All of the remaining yellowed teeth appeared in a wide-open grin. "Then we see."

One afternoon Michael opened the front door to an elderly couple. The well-groomed pair took a step back in unison, their wrinkles wrapping into a scowl. He stood before them in filthy undershorts, his scraggly heavily salted and lightly peppered beard frizzing out in all directions. His uncombed unshorn greasy hair was splayed all about his shoulders. Radish eyes squinted from hollowed sockets at the impaling sunlight. The woman looked away, while the man cleared his throat. Accepting that Michael wasn't about to say anything, he eventually stated, "Maybe we came at a bad time."

Michael shaded his weak eyes from the overbearing sun. "It's always a bad time. What do you want?"

"It would be easier to speak with you if you put some pants on."

"It be easier to speak with you if your false teeth weren't in backward."

"Sir, I don't have dentures."

"And I don't have any clean pants. What do you want?"

The woman turned back to confront him, rigidly locking her gaze on his face. "We're from the historical society." Michael scratched his balls. She sighed heavily, then pressed on. "We think you have done a marvelous job with this house. We would like to register it."

"It's not a house. It's a ship."

The man interceded. "Maybe we can set up an appointment for another time."

Michael yawned for ten seconds, repelling the old couple with his breath. "I'm pretty busy."

"We can tell," the woman leaned forward anyway, struggling to smile. "It's amazing what you've accomplished."

"Later." Michael slammed the door. The two elderly people looked at each other. Then walked back to their car and drove off.

The following morning Michael looked out a window of a third-floor room and saw Gerald drive up. Michael watched as he climbed out of his pickup and gazed up in awe. Gerald made a complete circuit of the house, gawking upward. New roof. All the exterior trim had been repaired. New glass in the windows. The porch had been rebuilt. The brick chimney had been repaired. The entire exterior was freshly painted, a white that shone in the sun.

Michael watched Gerald step up onto the front porch. Heard him pound on the door. "Hey, Mike!" Gerald bellowed. "It's Gerald! Open up!" He pounded some more. Then yelled some more. "The Whitfields were out here yesterday and they said you look really bad!" More pounding. "They said you were really rude, too! You've got no reason to treat them like that! They want to make your house a historical landmark!" Gerald pounded several more times. "Mike! Come on! You're scaring me!"

A moment later Michael heard the front door open. "Mike!" Gerald yelled. "I'm coming in! I hope you've got some clothes on!" Hearing the creaks of the stairs as Gerald climbed to the second floor, Michael ducked into a room on the third floor, then waited and watched as Gerald reached the third floor. "Mike. I've got to come up and check on you. I know you're here – your truck's out front. I'm coming up, so cover up." Gerald climbed the stairs to the tower room.

"She's not up there."

"Damn!" Gerald jerked around, sliding down the steps back to the third floor. "You scared the shit out of me."

Michael stood before him, with a stare black as a coal mine. "How long you been coming here? Seeing her?"

"Who the hell are you talking about?"

"I've been busy."

"I can see that. It's amazing…"

"Too busy to spend time with her. So you've been sneaking in here while I was working, seeing her."

"There's no woman here, Mike."

"I should never have given you that key."

Gerald reached into his pocket. "Here, you can have it back."

Michael jumped back, whipping out his pistol. "Get your hand out of your pocket!"

Gerald stepped back, raising both hands, one clutching the house key. "I was just returning your key. Mike, you need to calm down."

Michael lowered the gun, and sagged. "She's a beauty, ain't she?"

"Who?"

"Ligeia."

"I have no idea who you are talking about. Now put that gun away. You're going off the deep end."

"I've been deeper under the water than you could ever imagine."

"Now it's time to come up for air."

Michael smiled. "You should hear her sing sometime."

"I know," Gerald replied. "Loveliest voice I ever heard."

"Fucker!" Michael yanked the gun back up. "You have been with her!" He fired. Gerald collapsed on the floor.

* * *

Gerald had just climbed out of his pickup truck when he heard the gunshot. He reached under his seat to grab his gun, then ran up onto the front porch. He burst through the unlocked door. "Mike!" He dashed up the stairs, in the direction he'd heard the gunshot come from.

Clambering up to the third floor, he found Michael sprawled at the top of the stairs, the back of his head blown away. His gun lay on the floor nearby. Gerald recoiled in horror, looking all around. Not seeing anyone or anything about, he lowered his gun and pulled out his phone. But before he could call nine-one-one he heard the sweetest voice singing the most beautiful song he had ever heard.

ANNA IN THE NIGHT

John Mueter

When it was announced that he was a recipient of the prestigious Barton Prize for Composition, Ansgar Bjorn considered what he would do with the tidy sum of $25,000. It was not exactly a fortune, but it was nothing to sneeze at either. He realized that it could afford him many luxuries, or even frivolities, if he were so inclined. But being the well-disciplined and dedicated artist he was, he rejected the idea of a Caribbean cruise or a spiffy new car. He would reserve a cabin at the MacFadyen Retreat where he could compose, uninterrupted, for the entire summer and live in the company of other artists.

The MacFadyen Retreat is situated in the Adirondack Mountains of New York State, a place well known in the artistic community. It had been established sixty years before as a venue for artists of various disciplines – writers of fiction and non-fiction, poets, composers and visual artists – to live together in beautiful surroundings and pursue their individual projects in peace. It was far off the beaten track, assuring minimal intrusion from the outside world. The Retreat offered a quiet place to work and convivial fellowship when it was desired. Each participant was assigned a cabin, set off from the others, a short walk from the main house where meals were served and artistic communion could be enjoyed.

As a graduate student at the Juilliard School, Ansgar Bjorn had stayed at the Retreat once before, some twenty years earlier, the recipient of an academic grant. In his early years, he had been a young firebrand, an *enfant terrible,* intent on conquering the world of music. Since then, he had calmed down and had earned for himself a respected place in the select company of contemporary composers. It was quite an achievement for someone still in his mid-forties. His compositions had been performed by some of the top orchestras and chamber ensembles at home and abroad. He looked forward to three months of continued steady work on his latest commission, a piano concerto.

Knowing the lay of the land at the MacFadyen Retreat, he requested a specific one of the cabins, the one they called the Green House. It was one of the largest cabins, the one that was the most isolated from the rest, and came furnished with a decent piano – an old Steinway that would serve him well.

When he arrived in mid-June, quite early in the season, he was a bit taken aback by how slowly the season had progressed. It was still early spring up in the mountains. He was surprised and delighted to see a few tulips in bloom. The chilly temperatures were no problem – he knew he would be comfy in his cabin, and the boy scout in him looked forward to building a wood fire in the Franklin stove. After he was installed in the Green

House, he met the Retreat's other residents: a novelist, a poet, and two landscape artists. More would arrive later.

The Green House was so named because the inside pine walls were stained in a pleasing light aqua green. It was the oldest structure in the compound, built as a summer retreat by the original owners of the property. The building was constructed entirely of wood, with a vaulted ceiling over the main room. The cross beams were rough-hewn logs. Since there was no real foundation, the building had settled over the years and the bedroom floor sloped noticeably to one side. Ansgar loved the rustic, unpolished quality of the house and the fact that it was surrounded by a forest. The approach to it was by a narrow path, tricky to navigate even in daylight and treacherous in the dark. He imagined he could be content living and working in the seclusion of the Green House.

It was the third night of his stay when the first odd thing happened. Ansgar was a heavy sleeper and not easily aroused from his slumber. In the middle of the night he heard, or thought he heard, musical tones, sounds emanating from the piano: two notes played ever so gently at the higher end of the keyboard. At first, he wasn't sure if he were dreaming or if his ears were playing a trick on him. But, as he had perfect pitch, he was able to identify the notes as A from the instrument's sixth octave and the C above it. He soon fell back to sleep. By the next morning, he had forgotten all about it. He rose early, took his shower and dressed. Heading to the small kitchen area to make himself a cup of tea, he noticed that the lid of the keyboard was open. He always closed the lid at the end of the day. Always. It was a part of his working ritual. He stopped in his tracks at the sight of eighty-eight keys. The memory of the two notes flooded back into his consciousness. It was highly improbable that anyone could have snuck into his cabin in the middle of the night. Who would do such a thing? And why would they? It would be a strange joke to play on him. He considered that his artistic comrades might not be as solid as he thought.

By breakfast time, he managed to purge any concerns about the odd occurrence out of his mind. He sauntered down to the main house where he enjoyed a hearty breakfast along with stimulating conversation with his colleagues. He headed back to his cabin and worked strenuously all day with only a pause for lunch. By evening, his thoughts were filled with satisfaction at the progress he had made on the first movement of his concerto. The cadenza was so intricate and difficult he could barely play it himself. He imagined that the pianists tackling the piece in the future would curse him for writing such difficult music, then thank him for giving them such a bravura showpiece. The project was coming along nicely.

After dinner he read. Before turning in, he checked to see that the piano lid was indeed properly closed. He put a book on top of it just to be sure. Nobody would be messing with his piano tonight!

He slept soundly – until he heard once more, gently but unmistakably, sounds issuing from the piano, this time three notes: A, E flat, C. He was sure he was not dreaming. The sounds were real, and he was both fascinated and fearful. He sat up in his bed in the dark a long time, listening intently for other signs of movement.

There were none. He eventually drifted back into an uneasy sleep.

The following morning, he was apprehensive about entering the living room. When he opened the door, he saw that not only was the keyboard lid open, but the book was on the piano bench. This truly frightened him. He went weak in the knees and had to sit down. What could this mean? And then it hit him that A-E flat was a tritone, an interval regarded for much of history as 'the devil's interval'. It was not a comforting thought. He did not care to be the victim of some satanic mischief.

At breakfast, he sought out the one person he felt he could talk to, the amiable poet Margot Frisell. She had been resident at the Retreat many times and knew its history better than anyone. She was somewhat older and exuded the good-natured wisdom that sometimes comes with age. He approached the small table she occupied by herself. Margot was idly gazing out the window, lost in thought, probably converting the landscape into verse. Her disheveled mess of gray hair was held together in a bun with what looked like an errant chopstick. She wore an over-sized teal cardigan that had seen better days.

"Hi Margot," he began, "it seems to me that you're the most level-headed person around here." She looked bemused by the comment but said nothing. "I'd like to ask you something about the MacFadyen Retreat, if you don't mind."

"Sure. Fire away!" She gestured to the nearest chair and he sat down.

"Well, this is a bit strange, and I hope you won't think I'm going soft in the head, but something very odd has been going on in my cabin during the night, the past two nights actually. I've been hearing notes played on the piano, distinctive tones. I am sure I'm not imagining it. Even the piano lid, which I know was closed in the evening, was open in the morning. And I found a book moved to a different place. It's unsettling. It's downright terrifying."

"You're in the Green House, right? I'm not surprised."

"What do you mean by that?" he asked, alarmed. "Am I living in a haunted house?"

"Well, it could be that you are. The place has a history, one few people around here are aware of." She stopped to take a few sips of tea, then resumed her account. "When this property was owned by the Cronenbergs, they spent half the year in that cabin, until the worst of winter weather made it impossible to remain. Mr. Cronenberg was a minister, some offshoot evangelical sect – don't ask me which one. He was a real tyrant, especially with his only child, a daughter. Anna Cronenberg was by all accounts an exceptionally smart and talented girl. She was especially good at music. Her father did buy the Steinway for her, and I'll give him credit for that, but he was otherwise very strict and controlling of every aspect of his daughter's life. Mrs. Cronenberg was totally bullied into submission. Two things happened when Anna was eighteen: she fell in love with a local boy and she wanted to go to college to earn a degree in piano performance. She was good enough to do it, they say. The minister disapproved of the boy – not religious, wrong ethnic background – and pursuing a career in music was, he thought, unseemly for a female. He belonged to the school of thought that firmly believes that anything pleasurable must be sinful – you know the type, I'm sure."

"Unfortunately, I do."

She took another sip of tea, preparing herself to continue. "Well, there were also rumors of abuse of a sexual nature by the father – but no one knows for sure about that. And we never will know. At any rate, poor Anna became so despondent – and can you blame her? – that one night she tossed a rope over one of the support beams in the living room and succeeded in hanging herself. It was a sad business. Cronenberg sold the property soon afterward and the new owners, the MacFadyens, bought it and founded the Retreat. That would have been in 1958."

"You mean that someone committed suicide in my living room? I wish you hadn't told me that! But it puts my weird experience in a new light. The notes I heard were A and C, and that would correspond to Anna Cronenberg. Pretty creepy, huh? But last night I heard A-E flat-C. What does that mean?"

"Don't ask me – you're the musician! You can read all about the whole sordid affair in the library. There are scrapbooks with clippings from the time of the event. It was a big story out here in the sticks."

Ansgar thanked Margot for her help and headed straight for the library. It was a comfortable room, a bit old-fashioned, with armchairs and over-stuffed sofas. The shelves were overflowing with a diverse assortment of books and magazines. He found the scrapbook from 1958 at the bottom of a pile. The first news report he read began:

The daughter of Reverend Roland Cronenberg, Anna Sophie
Cronenberg, was found dead yesterday morning in their cabin
on Raquette Lake Road, apparently the victim of a suicide.

Along with the article there was a photo of the girl. She
was lovely, in a party dress. Her winning smile radiated
confidence in a life still full of hope and promise. It broke
his heart to realize what had befallen her.

Anna Sophie? Ansgar knew that in the German
musical nomenclature, where the names of flats are
formed by appending an 's', E flat was called 'es', and
Anna would have known that too. Anna Sophie
Cronenberg was A-E flat-C. The realization made his hair
stand on end. But at the same time, he suspected that
whatever spirit was visiting him, if it was a spirit, was
benign. He needn't fear being murdered in his bed by
some ghoulish creature wielding a dagger. He rushed back
to the dining room to share this newest bit of insight with
Margot. She was still sitting in the same place.

"I know what A-E flat-C denotes," he began breath-
lessly. "It's Anna Sophie Cronenberg! Do you think it
possible that her spirit is visiting me? And if it is, why?"

Margot produced a slight smile. "Well, I'm no expert
in the occult – not sure I believe any of it, if you want to
know the truth – but it would seem to me that, if it is the
spirit of Anna, she feels a kindred spirit in you. She may
just want some positive attention, something she got little
of during her lifetime."

This seemed to make sense to Ansgar Bjorn. He
thanked Margot for listening to him and for her sensible

comments. He returned to the Green House somewhat becalmed and threw himself into polishing the cadenza.

The following night nothing happened. There were no unexpected piano serenades to disturb his sleep and his peace of mind. The night after that, he intentionally left the keyboard lid up; he wasn't sure why. Again, in the depths of the night, he was awakened by the same motif, A-E flat-C, only this time it was played brashly, insistently. After a few repetitions it stopped. Again he sat up, all ears, and heard nothing further. He called out: "Anna Sophie Cronenberg, are you there?" Silence.

He thought about the story of Anna's life and her tragic end. He felt deep empathy for her. The more he thought about it, the more he saw the wisdom in the theory Margot had advanced. As wacky as it seemed to his rational self, it was just possible that Anna's spirit was sending him a message. Maybe it was true that she just wanted to be recognized in some way. He resolved to do something about it.

Having finished the first movement of his concerto he began the second, the slow movement. He would make it an homage to Anna Sophie Cronenberg by using the three-note motif as the basis of the piece. When he had finished composing the entire concerto and put the finishing touches on the orchestration, he wrote a dedication on the title page:

To my gentle friend A.S.C.
May she rest in eternal peace

The dedication would puzzle musicologists for decades to come. The Bjorn Piano Concerto was frequently performed, and the slow movement in particular was singled out for praise. One New York critic described that movement as "...the composer's most profound and hauntingly lyrical composition", a comment Ansgar found enormously amusing.

For the rest of his stay at the MacFadyen Retreat, Ansgar Bjorn slept wonderfully well every night. There were no more mysterious sounds emanating from the Steinway for the rest of the summer.

WHERE WE HIDE

Ali Habashi

Savannah was watching the game, because Roy was watching the game. Before she had shifted her attention to the screen, she had been staring at Roy himself, but after hours of glaring in his direction, she simply could not look at his face any longer.

Every part of him, this man she used to love, disgusted her. The scruff on his cheeks, the dirty shirt he always wore, even the slight muscle definition he'd managed to keep from his younger, more athletic years. Before he had begun to work on his beer belly.

Masculine, she had thought once upon a time. It had only been a few years since then, but it seemed like decades.

Lazy, she thought. *All of it.* If she didn't shave her legs or wash her clothes or eat healthy, she was an unhygienic slob. Why did Roy get a pass?

"Oh, come on! What was that?" Roy yelled at the television.

"Shut up, Roy," Savannah responded. "If it was you

on the field, you'd be carried out of that stadium in a body bag. So how's about you shut your ass up for once in your no-good, piss-poor, lying, cheating life?"

Roy ignored her. He'd been doing that ever since the last time they fought. Savannah had hated it at first. She'd cried and shouted and finally fallen silent herself.

Then she had started insulting him. She said all of the things that she had forced to the bottom of her throat for years. All the hurt and the anger and the hate spilled out of her in a dark roiling wave.

For the first time in a long time, she had felt good. With each cutting word she sent Roy's way, she felt more like she had before she met him. Confident, strong, capable. Roy was still ignoring her, but she didn't much mind anymore.

In fact, she preferred it that way.

The more she thought about it, the more she realized that not one useful or intelligent thing had ever come out of that man's mouth.

Roy clapped his hands to his knees in frustration as the commercials began to roll, then heaved himself to his feet with a grunt. He checked his phone, tapped out a quick response, and then stepped towards the hallway. Savannah trailed after him, only a few feet behind. Once they were in their room together, Roy thrust his arms into the closet and yanked one of his better shirts off of the hanger. He slipped into a pair of blue jeans and tennis shoes, and checked his hair in the mirror. Savannah leaned her head against the doorframe and glared at him as he hesitated for a moment. He scanned the room slowly, then pushed past Savannah before she could move.

"Jerk," she spat at him.

She followed him into the kitchen. What the hell else was there to do in this place? Roy began to rifle through the kitchen cabinets, looking for something.

"Where are they?" he muttered as he opened and closed each set of cabinet doors.

"Be more specific and maybe I'll tell you," Savannah commented. "My guess is you're looking for something that's right where it should be. You just don't help with nothing in this house, so you have no idea where that is, am I right?"

"Ah!" Roy pulled a box of garbage bags out from underneath the sink and strode back into their room.

"You're helpless," Savannah groaned as he began to circle the room. Roy snatched pictures of the two of them and tossed them on the bed, their frames clicking together in protest.

"Hey. Hey!" Savannah sped into the room, tried to slow him down. "What the hell do you think you're doing?"

He went back to the closet and yanked out an armful of clothes – her clothes – and added them to the pile.

"Roy!"

"Sorry, hun," he grunted as he worked, slowly but surely removing all traces of her from the room. "But you have *got* to go. I've got company tonight."

Savannah drifted back in shock as he began to stuff her discarded belongings into the garbage bags. She watched, frigid and silent, as he stalked through the house and removed her from it, bit by bit.

Rage quaked through every part of her as he worked. Her vision narrowed tightly, until there was only Roy, more disgusting than he had ever been. She pressed her nails into the flesh of her arms, tried to hold herself together as Roy swept several beer cans from the coffee table and into the same bag as her clothes.

It was like he didn't feel anything. It was like he was completely heartless.

"You…" she seethed. "You soulless bastard!"

She slammed her fists down onto the top of their old television set so violently that it flickered to life.

"Halloween is right around the corner and Walmart has everything you need to trick-or-treat in style!" blared the commercial.

Roy dropped the bag he was tying and swiveled his head towards Savannah as she backed up in surprise.

"Need supplies for the perfect pumpkin-carving party? How about some spooky decorations for the front yard? Costumes for the whole family? We've got you covered! With prices so low they're scary—"

The television clicked off. Roy tossed the remote back on the couch and ran a hand through his hair, glancing down at the bag.

"Christ." And with that he heaved the bag over his shoulder and went to dump it into the trash.

Savannah stood very still, then slowly looked down at her hands.

By the time Roy got back, Savannah was no longer by the television. She was hiding.

She knew it was stupid, hiding like a child, but she couldn't help herself. When she was younger and her mom and dad started yelling at each other, she would always clamber under the sink or slide under the bed or tuck herself in the folds of a curtain.

She would pretend that she was invisible, that she was in a room with two strangers and neither of them could see her at all. She practiced at silence, attempting to stifle even the sound of her own breathing. Savannah would hold her breath for as long as she could; then when her little inflated cheeks began to tremble and her thoughts started to get fuzzy, she would exhale, long and slow through her nose. She'd pull the air back through her lips and fill her lungs again, and wait. She wore soft socks that made her footsteps quiet on the tiles, and shuffled through the house so she wouldn't slip. Invisible.

When puberty had finally struck, and she sprouted into a gangly collection of stickish limbs, she mourned the loss of her small body more than most. It was harder to hide now, and when it was harder to hide it was harder to avoid getting pulled into her parents' fights. Savannah was forced to open her mouth and raise her voice in order to battle the din that she could no longer avoid.

The older she got, the fewer hiding places there were, until it felt as though there were none left at all. She missed being small; she missed pretending to be invisible.

Idiot, thought Savannah. *Back then all I saw every day was my mom and dad fighting, and I still believed in all of that prince charming crap. Still wanted a boyfriend when I was in middle school. Still flirted with all of those high school guys who didn't know shit about how to make a woman feel good. Still needed my own marriage material when the only marriage I'd ever seen up close was a disaster zone. Idiot.*

Roy opened the door mid-laugh, his hand splayed on the lower back of a woman with black wavy hair and purple lipstick that was too dark for her pale skin. Savannah tugged absently at her own blond hair, always so long and yet so much thinner than she had wanted it to be.

With a flare of hot jealousy, Savannah noticed that Roy's other arm was curled around a pumpkin, and the woman's hands were laden with orange and black shopping bags. They were celebrating a holiday together. They were probably even going to *decorate* together, something Roy constantly ridiculed and refused to participate in when they were together. Savannah realized then that it wasn't jealousy she was feeling. It was unfiltered *hate*.

"Are you sure you don't want help?" laughed Roy, gesturing to the bags in the woman's arms.

"Mmm-mmm," she shook her head. "I am a big girl and I can do it myself." She heaved the bags onto the coffee table and began to pull out bags of candy and decorations.

"Kimmy, toss me a bag of candy," Roy said as he grabbed two beers from the fridge.

"No! This is for the kids tomorrow. Now come here and play this with me."

"Come on babe," he whined, wrapping his arms around her from behind. "Please? Just one piece?"

"Babe"? Savannah bristled. *How long have they been together? Is that why—*

"Oh, fine, just one piece. But only because you're being such a good sport about Halloween." She popped open the beer, took a swig, then pulled a large black box out of one of the bags.

"I'm so excited, I've always wanted to play with one of these."

"What is it?" Roy asked through a mouthful of chocolate.

She held it up happily.

"A Ouija board? Babe, I knew you were bad news." Roy spoke as though he were joking, but Savannah knew the difference by now. His tone was just bordering on terse, his smile no longer natural. He did not find this turn of events amusing at all. She smiled grimly.

"Scared?" Kimmy teased, sweeping the bags from the table and beginning to liberate the board from its wrapping. Savannah watched a few dismembered zombie limbs roll from one of the bags and twitched.

Heartless.

Roy tensed as well, then swept the decorations back into the bag and dragged them to the other side of the couch, where they wouldn't be in his line of vision. Savannah lifted an eyebrow.

He's jumpy.

"Okay, before we start, do you have any candles?" Kimmy asked.

He just threw them all out, thought Savannah. *Along with my clothes and my pictures and everything else that might have indicated that a woman lives here.*

"I don't think so."

"What about that one?" Kimmy pointed to a small crowded shelf, where a drooping candle stood hidden in the shadow of an old trophy. She loped over and picked it up, rotating the label so she could read it.

"Gingerbread latte?" she smirked. "I didn't realize you had such refined tastes, Roy."

"I liked how it smelled."

Savannah could hear the terseness return to his tone, just beneath the lie.

Kimmy flicked a lighter to life and touched it to the pre-charred wick. Little shadows danced over her hand as she placed her fingers on the planchette and gestured for Roy to do the same.

"Remember, when the game ends we have to move this thing to the 'Goodbye' spot, or else something evil might come through the board while we're sleeping."

She looks so excited. Savannah wished she could warn her. She wondered if she could.

"Hello?" Kimmy asked. "Are there any spirits here with us tonight?"

"Babe—"

"Shush, I'm trying to make contact."

Roy was not having fun. His spine was ruler-straight, his fingertips white where they pressed the planchette. He was glancing between the candle and the spot where he had shoved the Halloween decorations and the bag of plastic zombie parts.

Savannah wanted to get closer, *needed* to get closer.

I am here. I am still here.

"Does anyone want to speak with us tonight?" Kimmy asked.

The planchette moved.

All three of the room's occupants gasped in triplicate as the planchette stuttered across the alphabet on the board.

"F-R-U-" Kimmy said.

"Babe—"

"-E-B-U-"

"Babe I really don't think—"

65

"-P-I-N."

"Babe!"

The planchette stopped moving, and Kimmy stared at what she had written down.

"Frundlebumpin? That's nothing! Come on spirits, give me something to work with here!"

Roy, whose entire body had seized up with anxiety, suddenly swiped the paper and read the word for himself.

"Frundlebumpin."

His shoulders relaxed and he began to grin. Then he began to laugh.

"Don't laugh! This is serious." Kimmy was attempting to pout through a smile of her own, but before long they were both laughing together. When they had stopped chuckling, they leaned together and began to kiss.

It didn't take long before Roy had hefted Kimmy onto the couch behind them. Grinding into one another, neither of them noticed that they had abandoned the Ouija board without saying *Goodbye*.

Neither of them noticed Savannah either.

She had stopped hiding as soon as they had abandoned the board. Once they were not crowded around it, their hands masking its intricacies, she had seen it for what it really was: a door. It was small, as the dimensions of a game board so often were, but it could be opened. It was unlocked. *They had left it unlocked.*

Perhaps this would not have been so useful to someone else, who would have only been able to reach through the board as far as their arm could stretch, but Savannah knew she would be able to go farther than most. She supposed she had Roy to thank for that. Following their last fight, he had unwittingly given her back the advantage that she missed from her childhood: the ability to hide anywhere she wished, tucking and folding her small frame under and between and among until she was completely invisible.

Their last fight had been about something stupid. That was the worst part.

They'd had larger fights before that, about the girls Roy would flirt with when Savannah was not with him, about the constant barbed comments he would fling her way whenever she was doing something he didn't like, about the affair she *knew* wasn't only in her head like he had tried to make her believe.

The last fight was about dishes.

Roy had slid one of his snide remarks her way, about the state she had left the kitchen in the night before. The words had erupted from her before she could think them through.

"Are you kidding me with that shit? I only left a *few* dishes in the sink, something you do *every day*, Roy. Hell, the only reason I left those dishes there is probably because I'd already washed some of yours and I was sick and tired of doing the dishes all day. Have you ever even washed a dish in your life, Roy? I don't think you have. If you ever did, it was before you met me and started using me as your damn maid."

"Alright, I get it! I'll do the dishes!" he huffed, leaving the couch and pushing past her into the kitchen.

"Well, I guess miracles really do—"

Savannah did not feel it the first two times the knife was buried in her. The third time the knife slid past her skin it was hot, and unbearable.

"*All done, babe.*"

She screamed, and she kept screaming. She screamed before she died, and she screamed after she died. All the way up until Roy had finished dividing up her body and portioning it into a few old gym bags. When the last of her had vanished under the tight teeth of a zipper, only then did she finally fall silent.

Savannah had kept talking to Roy, trying to prove to herself that she was still alive, or at the very least not trapped haunting the one man she could no longer stand to look at. Insulting him helped. There was no caution in her words anymore; there didn't need to be.

She was finally invisible

Roy had *made* her invisible. Roy had made her small. Most importantly, Roy had made her *many*. The Ouija board doorway was as bright as the flame cuddled in her old candle.

Savannah moved away from her hiding places, all of them.

Her legs dragged themselves from underneath the kitchen sink. Her arms dragged themselves out from underneath the couch. Her torso appeared from the end of the unlit hallway. Her hands dropped from the ceiling like spiders, caught in the stringy blond tresses of her hair as her severed head followed suit. If she were not invisible, then Roy and Kimmy would have been able to see her head, watching them from where it hung from the lighting fixture above, long blonde tangles wrapped around the bulbs until they glowed gold, her eyes never leaving them.

She crept inch over inch towards the doorway. It was too small for most spirits, but not for her. Her arms and legs went first, plunging through the board like fleshy tentacles. Her head and hands were next, fingers curling and hair twisting until they too were on the other side. Savannah knew that her torso would need to be left behind, but she didn't hesitate. She didn't need it anymore.

She collected herself above the board, arms and legs and head and hands loosely floating in their original positions, before she had been mutilated. The planchette she lightly plucked from the board and placed below her neck, where a heart might have been.

Savannah found that she could not speak, not without her torso, and so she waited.

Kimmy saw her first.

The expression on her face froze. Her jaw tightened and her eyes widened, but otherwise the shock held her motionless. Roy, his face buried in her neck, did not seem to notice the shift in the atmosphere, and continued to grind against her.

Savannah, slowly and deliberately, turned her accusing glare on Roy. Kimmy noticed.

"R-Roy?"

He finally glanced up and stopped moving as he registered the look on Kimmy's face. Slowly, he turned.

"Savannah?"

In a moment he had rolled off of Kimmy, his back pressing hard into the couch as though he were trying to escape through it.

As they stared at her puzzle-body with mounting terror, Savannah raised one severed hand and pointed at the man who lived in her house. It was an accusation, and a promise.

"You know her." Also an accusation. Kimmy was staring at Roy now too, and the fear in her voice was layered with miserable disbelief. The naked horror in his expression must have betrayed something deeper, because she very suddenly seemed to calm.

"Kim, don't—" began Roy, but Kimmy was already shaking her head. She stood, impossibly accepting, turned to Savannah and nodded. Savannah tipped her head in response. Kimmy's lips were pinched and quivering, her hands clenched into white-knuckled fists, but haltingly, she managed to lurch towards the door.

Roy was on his feet and rushing after her before the door had closed, but before he could catch up, blonde hair was twisting in bloody ropes around his head, and hands were peeling back his lips and working their way down his throat.

Savannah's fingers thrust into the narrow tunnel of his esophagus, tearing at the muscle there until they could stretch and flex. Her fingertips pressed their prints inside of his body, feeling at the wet workings.

Then, meticulously and piece by piece, she began to take him apart.

THE GARDEN

Sue Eaton

'It has a large garden by today's standards,' the woman gabbles brightly. 'It does have a mind of its own, though.'

You're a batty old woman, I think. I smile sweetly. 'A mind of its own? What do you mean?'

'It's a very old house, and I've found that it doesn't matter what I do, the only plants that survive are the old-fashioned ones – you know, ones that would have been growing when the house was built.'

'Really?'

'I don't mind. I think they make the property. I use the herbs anyway.' She stops and looks at me. 'You're on your own?'

'Yes.'

'No young man?'

'No. And no young female either.'

She colours but carries on without pausing for breath. 'It's just that it's a roomy cottage and the garden takes some looking after. That's why I'm selling. I don't really want to, but I can't keep it up by myself. Not at my age.'

'I have plans.'

She twists her neck so fast I think her head will drop off, and she stares at me in anticipation.

'For the house. And the garden.'

'Ooh, they won't like that.'

'Who? The house and garden?' I gasp.

She nods.

Nutty as a fruitcake. 'It wouldn't be straightaway. I'd need to get the feel of the place first.'

I had seen an article about hiring out your house to a film crew. You don't have to own a mansion or stately home. They need ordinary houses as well as interesting-looking ones, and this cottage is interesting in a Cheshire country sort of way. I'd been left a serious amount in my father's will. I could afford to buy this cottage and have money to spare.

It takes a bit of haggling, but I manage to secure the house for a decent price, leaving some money to put aside for improvements and leaving myself enough to live on for a few months whilst I concentrate on my writing. After a few weeks I move in.

* * *

It is so quiet here. I stand in the garden and listen. I cannot remember anywhere being this quiet. It's a pensive sort of silence as if someone is waiting in the shadows, ready to break it. I shudder in a cool breeze. Perhaps that's why the woman who used to live here talked so much. She needed to fill the silence.

'Hello?' a voice from the side of the hedge startles me. 'Are you the new tenant? I'm Barbara. I live next door. I've got the kettle on. I bet you're ready for a cup of tea. Are you planning on doing something with the garden? It's got a mind of its own that garden – if you'd believe such a thing.'

Dear Lord, not another one.

'Hello. I've bought the place, actually. My name's Tiffany.' No harm in using my pen name. 'I'm a bit busy at the moment, but I might take tea another day.'

'Oh, what have you got on?'

'I'm a writer. I've just come into the garden to mull over an idea and I don't want to lose the thread of my story.'

'A writer, eh? That's a new one for down here. We have all sorts in the village, you know. Footballers and everything.'

Orgasmic. I wave my phone in her general direction. 'Lovely. Excuse me my phone's buzzing. I'm expecting a call,' I lie.

* * *

I decide that I will modernise the back garden and have lots of decking and tubs with gravel between. People like that sort of thing and it's easy to get around with cameras and other paraphernalia. I ring round for quotes.

Bill 'No job too small' Weatherall arrives late, but at least he arrives, unlike Stan 'No job too big' Matheson. 'I thought I recognised the address,' Bill says scratching his cheek. 'Got a mind of its own, this place.'

'So I've been told,' I sigh. 'I can't keep this garden up

as it is, though, so what do you think?' I hand him my rough plans.

He draws in air through his teeth. 'Not to scale, these plans?'

Scale? 'Er, no. Is that a problem?'

'Don't suppose so. I'll have to measure it myself, though.'

It sounds like a problem. I don't hear from him again and he doesn't answer his phone.

'OutDoor Living Garden Services' is rather expensive, as is 'Country Gardens', so I decide to have a go myself, after all. I have to go to one of those out-of-town garden centre places to buy some tools. They don't come cheap, but they do come cheaper than 'OutDoor Living' and 'Country Gardens'

At first, I begrudge the time I have away from my writing, but I soon realise that it's quite pleasant outside in the warm sunshine and I can think about my novel as I hack away at the swathes of greenery.

I start on the front garden. I have been thinking and am not sure I want folk traipsing all over my property. I might just hire out the front, if that would work. It's rather pretty with its roses and ivy-covered walls.

The post lady catches me sloshing weed killer between the flags. 'Got a mind of its own, this garden,' she informs me as she hands me a pile of junk mail, all addressed to the previous owner. She nods at the weed killer. 'It looks like rain. That needs to go on twelve hours before rain.' *I know that.* So, I leave the front garden; it's lunchtime anyway.

Early next morning, wearing my oldest jeans and T-shirt, I put on my shiny new gardening clogs and matching gloves and head to the back garden to remove the overly large flowery thing that's blocking the sunlight. Where to start? I pull on a couple of the tentacles and realise that they disappear into the body of the flowery thing. I follow them until I feel a tightening around my ankle. I'm caught up in the damned thing and I nearly fall headlong. I just manage to grab at the trellis, but I break a nail, even through the gloves, hurt my hand and graze my forearm. The brand-new hedge trimmers crash to the ground and the handle cracks. A shadow passes over me and I hear giggling. It sounds like a child.

'Are you alright, dear? What are you doing?' Barbara is craning her head over the hedge.

I turn with a fixed smile on my face. 'I'm getting rid of this flowery bush.'

'The clematis?' She sounds horrified. 'That's very old.'

Time it went, then. 'I'm sure it is, but it's blocking the light.'

'It's nice and cool in the summer. Lily used to sit under it and read.'

'I caught my foot in one of its tentacles.'

'I think you mean tendrils.'

I know what I mean. 'Whatever. It's dangerous. I could have fallen.'

'It's not the right time for pruning. Anyway, I think it's holding the gazebo up.'

Gazebo? That old monstrosity? I glare at the building beneath it. A shadow passes through like a cloud passing over the summer sun. There's that giggle again.

My hand stings and I decide I've done enough gardening for one day.

* * *

Mug in maimed hand, I inspect the front garden the following day. The weeds are still healthy, but the climbing rose that grows where the ivy doesn't takes my attention. The flowers have been very pretty, but they are going over, and the dropped petals look untidy and tread into the house. It will have to go, I decide.

I consider chopping it off at ground level, but it appears to be firmly anchored to the wall and the flowery thing has taught me one lesson at least. I wrap myself up against the thorns and start to snip away at it with secateurs. Within minutes I find I am trapped by my hair. I try to pull away, but the pain makes my eyes water and I blunder into another overhanging branch, which gouges a furrow across my face and right eye. I feel someone brush past me making me shout out in panic.

My squeal brings a dog to my rescue. 'Hold still,' says a rich, warm voice. The dog's owner, I presume. I feel him begin to untangle my hair. It hurts as he pulls clumps of my hair free, but my reactions don't seem to faze him. 'Keep still, I said,' he mutters as he pulls and twists. 'There.'

Once I'm free, I turn to face him. He's no Prince Charming, then. He must be fifty if he's a day.

'It's quite a low hanging rose,' he says. 'You need to be careful. What were you doing, anyway? It's the wrong time for pruning.'

'I'm getting rid of it. The petals are a pain.'

'That's a good old rose. What on Earth do you want to get rid of it for? Just sweep the petals up.'

What business of this is his? 'I'm trying to alter the garden to suit me. Nothing is going right. I can't even kill the weeds.' I point to the lush green foliage between the flags.

'That's a herb. It's called 'heal-all'. It was once considered to be a Holy herb, sent by God to cure all ailments of man or beast, and said to drive away the devil. Some people thought that it was grown in witches' gardens, so people wouldn't be inclined to accuse them of witchcraft. You'll not get rid of that. Not here.'

Another nutcase as well as being a know-it-all. 'I'm no witch.'

'I should hope not. Unless… you really are, and the garden is trying to expel you,' he jokes.

'Don't say it, 'It has a mind of its own.''

'It might as well have.' He smiles and collars his dog. 'You take care. I'd have that scratch attended to. It looks nasty.'

It is nasty. I need to have a tetanus injection and a course of antibiotics. Meanwhile the garden goes rampant and the spiders' webs become so prevalent I begin to think I'm living in a fairy tale.

I give up on altering the garden as I have noticed that right at the back is a huge straggly bush with berry like things growing on it. By the time I wander up there they are turning red and look remarkably like huge raspberries. I love raspberries, so taking a colander I head for them.

'You've got a goodly crop this year.' Barbara is out in her garden. 'I love raspberries.'

'I'll pass you some over when I've picked them,' I promise, fingers crossed. *As if. I'm going to freeze them for later.*

I begin to get lost in the monotonous rhythm of picking while fleshing out the next chapter of my novel in my mind. The sun is warm and there is only the sound of the birds and a distant lawn mower to disturb me. I edge around the bush and fill my colander almost to the top. I take a step back and go backside over boobies, raspberries showering down on me like rain. My foot is stuck in a crevice in the old crazy-paving and I twist my ankle as I fall, cracking my left shoulder against the trunk of the pear tree on the way down.

I try to get up but feel so sick and dizzy that I lie back and hope that Barbara appears. She doesn't, but I hear the giggling again. Some little bugger can see me. After a while the dizziness recedes, although the nausea does not. To top it all, the pain sets in. I sit up and shuffle back from the crevice, managing to pull my foot out. The dizziness is back with increased nausea. The ankle looks a funny shape and the pain dims my vision until I think I pass out for a bit. The sun is blinding, and my head is beginning to ache. *Where the bloody hell is Barbara when you need her?*

I don't know how long I lay there but the sun has moved, or perhaps it's just someone in the way.

'Goodness, Tiffany, what have you been doing?'

'I fell.' My mouth is dry, and my voice sounds as if I haven't used it for a while.

'How long have you been there?'

'Ages.'

'Why didn't you call?'

'I did.'

'I've been out shopping, so I suppose I wouldn't have heard you.'

Really?

'What are we going to do with you?'

'I think I've broken my ankle. You might call an ambulance.'

'I don't like the look of that ankle. I'll call an ambulance. It might need seeing to.'

Why is it when you are in your oldest clothes, blotchy with sunburn and covered in twigs and squashed raspberries that they send the best-looking paramedic they can find?

They tell me my ankle is just badly sprained but keep me in overnight in case I have a concussion. The handsome paramedic doesn't come to see how I am. He probably isn't turned on by the dragged-through-a-hedge-backwards tramp look. Either that or he's gay.

'There was this gorgeous paramedic by the coffee machine as I came in,' my best friend, Kylie, informs me when she brings me some essentials. 'He's taking me to that new nightclub that's just opened in town.'

I smile sweetly. *Bitch cow.* 'Good for you.'

I arrive home to find the colander full of raspberries in the fridge, together with a fresh bottle of milk and a note from Barbara to say that she has helped herself to the rest of the fruit as it will only rot if left. Nipples, would they rot. I'd have put them in the freezer as planned.

Barbara is a bit of a godsend over the next week or so while my ankle heals. She helps with the shopping and keeps me company, which is not so good, but she does give me a bit of the history of this row of old cottages, which might prove useful if I am going to sell the idea of using mine to a film company.

Apparently, the cottages in this row had once been

alms-houses. My cottage, which is set back from the others, had originally been for the warden and had not only the earth closet for communal use (*ugh!*) but there had been a well in front.

'That would make a brill feature,' I enthuse.

'Lily's husband, God rest his soul, tried to find it when he was alive, but there was no sign,' Barbara tells me.

It doesn't put me off, though, and as soon as I feel up to it, I make a start. The front garden is quite small, so it shouldn't take too long. First to go is the standard rose in the centre. I mean, it stands to reason that the well was in the centre of the plot.

Barbara is not convinced. 'They dug this all over, you know. Didn't find a thing. It will have been filled in ages ago. Health and safety and all that.' She hands me a mug of tea.

I am determined to find the old well if I can. It's beginning to become a bit of an obsession, and the next morning finds me up early digging over the patch trying to find some evidence.

'You'll do yourself a mischief, Tiffany.' I don't look up at first, forgetting that I gave Barbara my pen name rather than my real one. 'Tea?' she adds. I do look up at that.

'Thanks, Barbara. I could do with a cup. Just let me level this off.'

'You'll do no such thing. The tea is here. Drink it. You look dreadful.'

'Thanks for that!'

'Well, you do. You've been at it all day.' I hold out my hand for the mug. 'And just look at those blisters. Call it a day, Tiffany. Enjoy the weather while it lasts.'

I sit on the wall beside her while we drink, but as soon

as she leaves to watch her afternoon soaps I start again.

A shadow passes over the hole I am digging and I hear a giggle. I look up to see a slight young girl watching me. She looks a tad scruffy in an old-fashioned sort of way and the overall impression is of green. 'You'll not find it there.'

'Find what where?'

'You're looking for the well, aren't you?'

'How do you…?'

'I make it my business to know what happens in this house.'

'Why?'

'I used to live here. Way back when.'

'And the well was here then?' I realise what I've said. 'But Lily and her husband lived here for years and they never saw the well.'

'They didn't look.'

'Of course, they looked. Barbara told me they looked.'

'Not really looked. They never noticed me. I would have told them.'

'Okay. So, tell me.' She moves to the edge of the garden.

'It's here.'

'Under the path?'

'Under this corner of the path. Handy for all the folk in the row.'

'Oh, I just thought…'

'That it was central? No, you build the well where the water is.' She pulls a forked stick from her belt and holds it out over the spot she has indicated. The stick waves up and down. It's my turn to giggle. What a performance. 'Here.' She looks at me. 'Dig here.'

Why I would take any notice of a young girl who is obviously telling me a tale, I will never know. Lily is ancient. There's no way this child could have lived here before she did. But I feel myself compelled.

The soil in the bottom of the new hole soon turns to sand and then starts to become wet. Slowly the dampness turns to water. I keep digging. The girl keeps watching.

Suddenly I feel the ground shake a little under my feet. Instead of concern, I find I am becoming excited at the prospect of actually finding what I'm looking for. My thought as I plunge through the ever-broadening hole is, *I've found it. The well.* Blackness covers the light from the sun, and I feel a sigh as my breath leaves my body. I can't breathe. It is then I start to panic and struggle, but the action only pushes me deeper into the wet. Lights flash across my eyes, but my vision is darkening. I try to draw in oxygen, but the garden won't let me. The last thing I hear is a tinkling giggle far above me in the darkness.

PERSONAL DEMONS

Phillip Drake

Ricky decided to drive home, despite the three pints of lager and a single malt whisky he had downed before leaving the Half Moon pub. The rugby match had gone well, the lads putting in a stellar performance to beat 'that lot' from the next town. It had been their first victory over their rivals for ten years, and the drinks had flowed freely upon return to their familiar watering hole.

Opening the door to the street, frigid air licked his face and instantly seemed to penetrate deep beneath his thick woollen coat; and for a moment or two he almost gave in to the shouts from his teammates to stay for a few more. He was surprised to see the snow, which had already given the pavement and the tops of the cars a substantial coating. It hadn't been forecast, despite the falling temperatures.

In the sodium glow from the nearby streetlamp, the continuing snowfall whirled in the breeze before it fell to the ground to add depth to the existing layers.

This is just like that night a few years ago, that night when...

Before his mind could replay more dark images, the pub door slammed shut behind him bringing him instantly back to the now, yet gossamer after-images remained, set free by the alcohol and his own senses.

Ricky stepped down onto the pavement. The effect of the alcohol and the slippery snow-covered path slowed his progress to his vehicle, the minibus he had hired to take the team to their match. Now it was his job to return it to the hire company's yard before collecting his own car and driving home.

Upon reaching the vehicle, Ricky wiped the accumulated snow from the driver's side window, before pressing the keyfob that unlocked the doors with a satisfying clunk. He was about to wrench the door open when he thought he heard a sigh coming from behind him. Thinking one of his teammates had crept up on him without him noticing, he spun around but there was nobody there. He stood watching as another deep sigh seemed to send a few big lazy snowflakes spiralling off in intricate patterns before they settled.

Ricky turned back to the minibus, hastily opened the door and climbed up into the driver's seat. He closed the door quickly and then locked them all. Shivering despite the warming effects of the alcohol, he turned the heating up to the maximum as soon as he had started the engine.

He gazed momentarily at his hands on the steering wheel, pale and lined with age, the skin not as taught as it once was. He noticed a slight tremor.

It was just the wind; that's all, just the wind.

He felt tired, drained even, and his memory kept trying to replay those images he didn't want to see. The game had taken a lot out of him, and combined with the drink and the lack of sleep, his body yearned for rest. He hadn't slept well for some time; the dreams had returned, but then they always did at this time of year, and with them came insomnia and anxiety.

Ricky rubbed at his eyes as if to wake himself and turned on the radio, auto-seeking through the stations until he found something that he liked. Eventually he hit upon one playing an old familiar song from decades past, which brought back different memories, pleasant ones this time. He smiled, switched on the headlights and the windscreen wipers and was ready to go.

The roads were quiet even for a Sunday evening, but Ricky figured that with the worsening weather people had probably decided not to venture out. He'd only been driving for a few minutes when his phone rang, the hands-free Bluetooth system built into the minibus connecting the call almost instantly.

'Hi hun. Where are you?' The familiar voice of his wife Janice.

'I'm just on my way to return the minibus – then I'll be home. It shouldn't take more than an hour,' he replied.

'Just be careful. The weather's getting worse, and I've just heard on the radio that the motorway has been closed due to an accident,' she said, and Ricky could detect a hint of concern in her tone, despite the slight distortion of her voice through the speakers.

'Great, that's all I need,' he replied, cursing under his breath at the news of the motorway closure and looking to see whether the radio in the minibus had traffic alerts turned on.

'How will that affect your journey, hun?' Janice asked, her concern now even more evident.

Ricky sighed heavily. 'I'm not sure. I'm going to have to take the back roads. It'll take longer, and that's if they're passable with this snow.'

There was no doubt that the weather conditions had deteriorated even in the few minutes since Ricky had left the relative safety of the pub car park. Even with the windscreen wipers on full speed, visibility was poor.

'Well okay, just take it slow and if you get into difficulty call me,' Janice replied. Her soft delicate voice was of great comfort to him, but at the same time made him yearn to be at home with her and their two girls.

'I sure will,' he said, hoping that his simple reply was enough to reassure her, and with that, they said their goodbyes.

It took a few more minutes before Ricky reached the junction that led on to the motorway, and sure enough, the blue flashing lights of the police car that was blocking the slip road told him that using the motorway was not going to be an option.

Diversion signs led on to the nearest B-road, a road he had often used in his youth, preferring it to the motorway back then, when his inexperience kept him nervous of motorway driving and convinced him that the 'scenic' route was safer. In these conditions, negotiating the bends and curves of this meandering road would be even more challenging than normal.

After travelling just a couple of hundred yards, Ricky soon realised that his vehicle was the only one on this sparsely lit stretch of highway, his only human company being the insufferable cheerfulness of the radio DJ.

Further on and this thirty-mile stretch of road was at least four inches deep in crisp white snow. The ruts of vehicles that had passed before now almost completely re-filled, and Ricky had to reduce his speed to a mere crawl.

As the conditions worsened, he had to wrestle with the steering wheel in order to keep the minibus straight, its tyres struggling for grip, spinning and whining as it made almost pedestrian-paced progress along a road that was rapidly becoming like it was a toboggan run.

Then he saw her.

A young woman wearing a thin white dress, one that was totally unsuitable for the conditions and made her seem almost camouflaged against the wintry backdrop. She stood in the snow almost motionless as if waiting to cross.

No, it can't be!

As he drew nearer, Ricky could see the woman's long dark hair. Lank and almost lifeless, it hung in long strands almost completely covering her features before ending just above her chest.

I'm tired; my mind is playing tricks.

Panicked by what he saw, Ricky pushed gently down on the accelerator, and as he passed the figure of the woman, she looked up at him, and they made eye contact – only there were no eyes for Ricky to look into. Where the eyes should have been there was nothing but blackness, deep soulless depressions in milky white skin, accompanied by a half-smile on thin pale lips.

The extra speed caused the minibus to career recklessly down the narrow lane, Ricky not easing his foot from the accelerator pedal despite the danger. Thin branches of hedges flayed against the side windows as the tyres carved grooves into the ice and snow.

Ricky grappled with the steering wheel as the minibus slid around a gentle bend in the road, but the next bend was a tighter one, a road sign warning of its approach, and despite his best efforts, the bus wasn't going to make the turn.

A tree-lined hedge loomed up, and the minibus sped through before slamming to a sudden stop in a ditch, one that Ricky hadn't seen, but which had saved the bus from hurtling headlong into a tree. The force of the impact threw Ricky forward, the front airbags deploying in a millisecond, their presence preventing his head from smashing through the windscreen. The engine revved then died, and then all was quiet.

Ricky stayed motionless for a moment, eyes closed, his mind trying to pinpoint any painful parts of his body that may give a clue to how badly he was injured. His face felt sore from the friction burns from the airbag, and he could feel a small trickle of blood from his left nostril, but everything else seemed intact.

A swishing noise from outside made him open his eyes. Was there someone there? Had someone witnessed the accident and come to lend assistance?

He couldn't help but replay the vision of the woman at the side of the road, the gaunt figure, the pale skin, the black void where the eyes should have been.

It was her; I know it was her.

'Hello…hello, is anyone able to speak to me?' The unexpected sound of a woman's voice jolted Ricky back to the present, and it took a few seconds for him to realise that the minibus must have been fitted with a system that automatically contacts the emergency services in the event of a crash.

'Hi…yes I'm here.' Ricky's voice was soft and carried a hint of desperation and panic. If nothing else, he knew it was inevitable he'd now lose his licence – with what he'd drunk earlier, there was no doubt at all that he'd be over the drink drive limit.

'Are you seriously hurt?' the woman asked.

'No, just a bit shook up.'

'How many people are in the vehicle?'

'Just me,' Ricky replied, although he couldn't be sure that was going to stay that way for much longer.

'Well, don't worry. We have your coordinates, and the emergency services are on their way to you.' Her voice was calm and reassuring. 'I'll stay on the line until they arrive.'

Ricky was about to thank her when he saw the face in the rearview mirror. The same face he had seen just moments before. This time it was peering in through one of the back windows. Ricky twisted round, opened his mouth – whether to scream or to protest was of no consequence, for no sound emanated from his constricted throat.

He watched as the figure silently made its way along the side of the minibus towards the front passenger door. In his panic, Ricky's instinct was to flee rather than remain in the minibus as the awful thing came towards him. He fumbled at the door handle, but it refused to open.

Remembering that he had locked the doors just prior to leaving the pub car park, he managed to unlock the driver's door, drawing in a sharp breath that might easily have been a sob when he felt it give.

Almost falling through the open door, Ricky launched

himself through the branches of the hedge, his clothing snagging on the sharper ends, whilst others scratched at the skin beneath. He thought he heard dry rasping laughter coming from the minibus behind him.

'Hello caller, are you still there? What's happening?' The call handler's voice carried on the frigid night air.

Ricky's only reply was a low moan as he tried to scramble out of the ditch to the road above. Trembling so violently that his fingers scrabbled against the snow-covered grass bank, it took him several attempts before he found enough grip to haul himself out.

Although he dared not stare directly at the vehicle, his head half-turned as if irresistibly lured so that he caught movement in his peripheral vision. He was sure what he had just seen was the female figure emerging slowly from the minibus.

Ricky's chest heaved. The call handler's voice was still asking for a response, but all he could emit from his throat was a terrified wail. He wanted to run from there, to flee before the approaching form reached him; yet he suddenly felt so lethargic, so somnolent, a dread-filled heaviness sinking through his limbs, clawing at his strength.

Without looking, he knew she had reached the bottom of the ditch, and he knew that she wouldn't have the same difficulty in negotiating the slope, for this woman was not of this Earth, at least not anymore.

For the first time, Ricky noticed a cottage only a few yards across the road. It was in total darkness, but it could offer sanctuary, and it gave him somewhere to go, somewhere other than here.

He could sense her behind him now, and he could feel

the warmth in his skin and veins drain from him, leaving his body leaden and cold. When he fled, it was with an awkwardness that wasn't just due to the conditions underfoot. His feet barely lifted from the ground and he lost his footing several times before making it to the front gate.

She told me she would get me.

Ricky thrashed at the front door with both fists, ignoring the shuddering shocks that ran up both arms. He tried to call out, but a terrible tautness in his throat muscles prevented him from doing so. All he could manage was a primal grunt as his blows against the door began to slow and become less hopeful.

Taken by surprise, Ricky almost lost his balance as the door suddenly opened inwards.

There was nothing welcoming about the old woman's demeanour. She opened her mouth to speak, but before any words could form Ricky had already pushed past her into the hall.

'Thank God you're in,' Ricky gasped. He was bent over, his hands resting on his knees as if he had just completed running a marathon rather than just a few yards.

Realising the old woman hadn't shut the door, another wave of panic washed over him.

'For God's sake – the door!' he shouted, and before she could react he pushed the door shut behind him, its traditional Yale lock automatically locking it shut.

'May I ask who you are and what you are doing here?' she asked him, her own voice hushed.

'Never mind that.' Ricky's reply was unintentionally brusque.

She'd never believe me.

'Is someone after you?'

'You could say that…' Ricky panted, but then decided it would be better not to try and explain what he had run from, better if he tried to make the situation at least sound normal. 'Look, I…I've had a road accident,' he said with a level of calmness that surprised even him. 'The emergency services are on their way. I just need to wait here until they arrive.'

'Oh dear, how awful,' replied the old woman. Apparently, calmness had been restored and, now at least, she didn't seem disturbed by Ricky. 'You'd better come and sit down, and I'll put the kettle on.'

She showed him into her living room, and Ricky felt reassured by the normalcy of his new surroundings and relieved to be there, even if he now felt a bit guilty about barging in on this old woman.

Before he could settle, though, a gentle drumming sound suddenly caught his attention.

He jolted as if something had touched him and pinned himself to his chair in fright.

The knocking on the door hadn't been loud, but to Ricky it felt as though the door had been shaken in its frame by thunderous, vigorous blows – the barrier straining against its hinges, the wood seeming to curve inwards, as though something was applying great pressure from the other side.

Ricky visualised the bulging door, its creaking groans discordant in the still hallway.

Suddenly the pressure from outside ceased.

'I'd better open the door,' the old woman chirped.

To Ricky's horror, he saw the woman shuffle out towards the hallway.

He got to his feet and headed after her. 'No, don't let it in!' he implored.

The old woman hesitated. She looked at Ricky, then back at the door. 'Don't be so silly. It's just my daughter.'

For the first time, Ricky took in the row of framed photographs adorning the walls of the hallway. Dust covered and faded with time, the photos were of the old woman in her younger days with a young girl. A girl Ricky knew very well.

With a movement that was astonishing in its rapidity, the old woman flung the door open. A shadowy figure stood outside. The old woman stepped back as the figure crossed the threshold into the dimly lit hallway, but even in the feeble light, Ricky could recognise the face.

When he fled, it was awkwardly, the soles of his shoes scraping across the bare floorboards as he made his way towards the rear of the cottage. He stumbled as he passed through the kitchen, his legs, weakened by fear, barely able to adjust in time to keep him from falling.

The door that led to the back garden and the fields beyond thankfully had its key in the lock. In his haste, Ricky fumbled with the lock, but after a couple of tries he had the door unlocked and he raced through the opening, out into the dark snowy night.

He thrashed through the snow-covered undergrowth, falling, rising, never stopping. Cruel branches whipped at his face and hands, snagging his clothes, concealed obstacles tried to trip him, but Ricky kept on running – never once tempted to look back, afraid of what might be following him. He reached the low fence that separated the garden from the field beyond and vaulted the low barrier like an Olympic sprinter.

He raced on through the snow-covered field, stumbling but somehow keeping his balance despite the treacherous conditions underfoot. Finally, he spotted a break in the landscape ahead, a large metal gate that led back on to the road.

After climbing it with great care – the metal sticky with ice burned his hands and fingers – Ricky allowed himself a brief moment to regain his breath, listening for pursuers as he did so, but all seemed quiet back there.

Then he felt the breath on the back of his neck.

Ricky spun around and jumped back almost in one movement. His back collided with the metal gate, the impact causing it to rattle noisily in its frame. He looked at the figure in front of him. Her face was no more than six inches from his, and he could do nothing but stare into those black voids where her eyes should have been. Her matted hair hung in limp strands against her pale almost bloodless skin, and as she moved closer, Ricky noticed the bluish-purple line around her throat for the first time.

He let out a barely audible cry as he attempted to retreat from her advance, but the rungs of the gate pushed back into his spine, the pain coursing up his back.

He closed his eyes as if in prayer.

She whispered his name.

'Leave me alone!' he shouted, hysteria close enough to raise the pitch of his voice. 'Just leave me alone!'

His cry became lamenting, almost a moan, as he sank to his haunches.

'Just leave me alone…'

The whispering stopped.

Then silence.

After a few seconds, Ricky felt a hand on his shoulder, and cautiously he opened first one eye and then the other.

Standing there was a man in a police uniform, the radio on his chest sporadically crackling into life as he bent over to get a better look at Ricky's face.

He pressed a button on his radio. '6599 to control…I've found him…about a hundred yards from the scene of the accident.' He let go of the button and a garbled reply came back, but Ricky couldn't make out any of the words.

'Are you okay, sir? Are you hurt at all?' The police officer shone his torch in Ricky's face, the light making him turn his head to one side so that he was looking sideways through the gate.

'She's out there,' Ricky breathed.

'I'm sorry sir?' The police officer looked puzzled, fearing that there may be another injured party somewhere. 'Was there somebody with you?'

A maniacal laugh came from somewhere deep inside Ricky as he stood up to face the police officer, and in one movement, he grabbed the officer by the lapels of his jacket and drew his face close so that their noses were almost touching.

'I killed her, don't you understand?' raged Ricky, his grip tightening as the officer tried to press the panic button on his radio. 'Twenty years ago, I murdered a woman and buried her in the field just over there.' Ricky nodded his head in the direction to where the minibus lay abandoned in its ditch.

The officer shrunk away, unsure of how to respond to

this sudden change of events, whilst Ricky continued with his confession.

'She was going to ruin everything, don't you understand?' The merest smile touched his lips. 'I was about to get married, but she wanted to get back at me for leaving her. She couldn't understand that she was just a final fling, you see?' Ricky could barely finish the sentence; the words caught in his constricted throat as tears rolled down his cheeks, two decades worth of guilt erupting to the surface.

'I offered to drive her home,' Ricky continued. 'She kept on and on about how we were meant for each other, so I stopped the car and the next thing I know my hands are around her throat.' Once he'd set these words free, Ricky eased his grip on the policeman and his head drooped to his chest.

Immediately, the officer took the opportunity to regain control of the situation, to get this mad man in cuffs and call for back-up. He led the now-subdued Ricky away down the snow-covered lane, and the sound of their feet crunching the snow underfoot was soon interrupted by the distant sound of more sirens.

* * *

The clouds have parted now, as the moon shines down on the largely neglected cottage. The building seems desolate, unloved, uncared for, the interior cluttered with shadows. However, someone stirs in the darkness, journeying from room to room, a woman of late years humming a jaunty tune, whilst waiting for her daughter to come home.

SWIM AT YOUR OWN RISK

Matthew Gorman

The trip to Rome had been a bumpy one. Overcome by exhaustion, Mrs. Worthington flopped onto the gilded bedspread and affixed her sleeping mask while her husband paced neurotically about the spacious suite commenting upon its amenities.

"Darling, please," she scolded him. "The flight was simply atrocious, and if I don't get a nap in before dinner I'll be a complete disaster."

"Well, don't sleep too long, turtle dove. We have reservations at Il Paradiso at eight, and you know how much I've been dying to try their *taglierini con tarufi*," Mr. Worthington said, over pronouncing the Italian like he always did.

"Yes, I am well aware of our reservation, darling."

"It's supposed to be the best in all of Rome, even better than the one they do at La Pergola. Did you know they actually have the truffles sent in daily from Alba, dear? That certainly must cost them a pretty penny."

"Chester Worthington," she said, speaking as if a

mother to a wayward child. "Surely, there is something with which you might occupy your time while I take a short rest. Doesn't this hotel have a casino or something, darling?"

"I'm afraid there are no casinos within Rome, my dear. In fact, I believe that there are only five land-based casinos in all of Italy and, sadly, none of them here in the city. A shame, as you do know how much I enjoy my baccarat."

"Yes, yes. Well, something then, darling. I really must sleep and that's quite impossible to do with you standing there yammering on and on about gold-plated bathroom fixtures and imported truffles. Surely, you must see that?"

"Yes, my dear. I'm sorry, my love. Actually, I'd thought I'd be up for a little swim. Did you know that the Palazzo d'Oro boasts one of the first indoor Olympic-sized swimming pools in the world? In fact, several members of the Italian national swimming team even used the hotel pool as a training ground in their preparation for the 1960 Summer Games right here in Rome. Quite fascinating, wouldn't you say?"

"I most certainly would not. A pool's a pool. So go, go, swim, swim," Mrs. Worthington mumbled, the half of a Valium she had taken at check-in already starting to work its magic.

"Of course, dear," Mr. Worthington said, and went to fetch his swimming trunks.

By the time he left the hotel suite, shutting the door gently behind him, his wife was already snoring peacefully away.

* * *

Mr. Worthington made his way to the basement level of the hotel where the pool was housed. A few dozen laps ought to be the very thing to work up an appetite for the rich pasta that he planned to consume at Il Paradiso tonight.

He located a small but richly appointed changing room just off the pool's main entrance and there he traded his shoes, shirt, and linen trousers for a pair of electric blue swimming trunks with a red racing stripe down either thigh. He drew his fitted neoprene swimming cap over his balding head, attached his purple silicone nose clip, and donned his anti-fog goggles before leaving for the pool. Mr. Worthington was a rather capable swimmer and with all his fancy accoutrements he felt he truly looked the part.

Ready to swim, he stepped out barefoot into the pool's natatorium and found himself instantly struck with awe. As the Chief Financial Officer for a Fortune 500 company for nearly two decades before his retirement, Mr. Worthington was accustomed to a certain standard of luxury, particularly when he traveled Europe, but the opulence of the pool and its environs were far and away above most that he had seen.

Inlaid pillars of pink marble rose high to meet the vaulted ceiling adorned with intricate frescoes of cherubs and angels that called to mind – quite intentionally, no doubt – those of the Sistine Chapel as they gazed down upon the water below. The floor surrounding the pool was wrought in a chessboard pattern of alternating Italy pink marble and stunning white Calcutta marble veined with gold, while potted palms thrust their fronds from intermittent alcoves along the walls to lend a hint of lushness to the massive room of metamorphic rock.

And the pool, itself, was a perfect shimmering field of turquoise blue that stretched the length of the enormous space with wispy white tendrils of steam rising up from its heated water.

But despite the grandeur of the room, there was an unsettling quality about it that Mr. Worthington couldn't quite put his finger on. It certainly didn't help that the only source of light came from a pair of crystal chandeliers suspended from the muraled ceiling high above. They bathed the room in a subdued and somber light where shadows hung from the corners like dark draperies. Nor did it help that he appeared to be the room's sole occupant. It seemed rather odd to him that none of the hotel's other guests had been up for a mid-afternoon swim.

And then there was the sign.

Affixed to the far wall was a white metal signboard, oddly unremarkable amidst the lavish décor, which provided a familiar warning in Italian: NO LIFEGUARD ON DUTY. SWIM AT YOUR OWN RISK. It was a notice he'd seen in many languages and at many a pool throughout the world, but here for some strange reason it struck an ominous chord.

But Mr. Worthington was here to swim, and he wasn't about to let some silly sense of unease put a stop to his plans. It was likely to pass once he found himself in the water, anyway.

The soles of his bare feet padding against the ornate tile, he approached the edge of the pool. Even with his nose guard in place, the smell of chlorinated water hung heavy in the air. It filled his mind with fond memories of a childhood spent swimming in the pool at his grandfather's estate in Portola Valley, and did much to assuage his unquiet nerves.

He dangled one foot over the edge and plunged his toes into the water to test its warmth. Olympic racing pools were generally heated at anywhere from 77 to 82 degrees Fahrenheit, and it seemed the Palazzo's pool certainly fell somewhere within this ballpark. It would make for an undoubtedly pleasant swim.

Taking care – though still strong of upper body, his knees weren't what they used to be – Mr. Worthington lowered himself into a sitting position with his legs submerged before sliding his buttocks across the tile to come to a full stand upon the bottom of the pool's shallow end.

He stood there for a moment enjoying the heat of the water against the paunch of his belly, his palms fanning to and fro across its surface. The far end of the pool looked truly far away and he was deciding whether it was best to swim his laps by employing the less exhausting breaststroke or by sticking with his usual forward crawl when he heard a child's voice addressing him from somewhere nearby.

"You going for a swim, mister?"

Startled, he spun in the direction of the sound, the water churning up around him like a boat's wake. There, he was surprised to find a young girl, no older than eight or nine, seated demurely upon the edge of a waterproof chaise lounge staring down at him from poolside. Where had she come from? he wondered. Had he simply missed her when he'd first come in, or had she been hiding until now as part of some frolicsome child's game?

"Uh…hello," Mr. Worthington said.

"Hello," the girl replied. Her eyes were wide and prepossessing but somehow quite sad.

"You're American?"

"Yes," she said. "From Philadelphia."

"Myself as well," he told her, smiling as warmly as he could. He'd never been too comfortable around children. "From the Bay Area. In California."

"Oh, I always wanted to go to California, but we never did."

"Well, you're young. Still plenty of time for that, I'd wager. Besides, you're in Rome – that must be very exciting," he said, trying his best to sound encouraging.

When the girl declined to reply, Mr. Worthington felt his uneasiness begin to grow once more. It was more than just the usual awkwardness he felt in the presence of the very young; there was something most peculiar about this particular little girl.

For one thing, her skin was unusually pale. In fact, it appeared almost translucent in places, the light blue veins in her forehead visible beneath the flesh. He wondered somewhat morosely if the poor thing might actually suffer from anemia. His former company had once manufactured a ferrous gluconate supplement to help combat the disease, and he'd become familiar with its symptoms.

A head of jet-black hair pulled tightly back from her face by an elastic tie or some similar device offset her milk-white skin, and the one-piece bathing suit she wore was a similar shade of ebony. Mr. Worthington thought her swimming attire appeared to be well made but – his snobbery getting the better of him – horribly out of fashion. Quite possibly she hailed from one of those formerly affluent families whose wealth was now in a state of gradual decline.

"Are you here with your parents?" he asked, uncomfortable with the silence.

"I came here with my grandmother, only I don't know where she is right now."

How wholly irresponsible, he thought, to leave a child so young completely unattended in a foreign country. And by a pool, no less. Of course, he could recall plenty of unsupervised swims at his grandfather's pool when he wasn't much older than this one.

"I'm sure she'll be along shortly. What's your name, child?"

"Elise."

"Why, that's a lovely name, isn't it? Well, Elise, it's a pleasure to make your acquaintance. My name is Chester."

"Pleased to meet you, Chester."

Such proper manners, he thought, perhaps there was indeed still hope for the youth of today. It seemed a shame that such a polite little girl ought to appear so lonesome and dejected. But that was hardly his concern.

"Well, it's been lovely chatting with you, Elise, but I really must get my daily regimen of exercise now. At my age, this isn't getting any smaller," he said, patting his gut beneath the water.

"If you're going for a swim, Chester, you should stay away from the deep end."

"Is that what your grandmother told you? I do suppose that's rather sound advice for little girls, Elise. But you see, I'm a grown-up, and grown-ups are allowed to swim in the deep end."

"It doesn't matter. You just shouldn't go down there."

"And why is that, sweetheart?"

"Because that's where the bad man lives."

Children and their fanciful imaginations, he thought. Still, he couldn't blame her for making up some sort of game to pass the time while she waited for her grandmother to return. Chances were the old woman was sitting half-soused on gin martinis or Campari sanguineas in the hotel lounge.

"That's funny because I don't see anyone down there now, Elise," he said, electing to play along.

"He hides," she whispered.

"Well, I'll be sure to keep an eye out for him," Mr. Worthington said with a chuckle, hoping to lighten the mood.

But the girl only stared at him with her sorrowful eyes.

Having had his fill of this conversation and wishing to begin his swim, he bid her a pleasant day and turned to face the length of the pool. But as he prepared to shove off from the wall, a thought occurred to him. Perhaps he should help the poor child in locating her neglectful grandmother, maybe giving the old woman a piece of his mind in the bargain. He was certain that the friendly, if overly talkative, front desk attendant could aid him easily in this endeavor. He'd have to change back into his clothing, of course – it certainly wouldn't do to have him go traipsing around the Palazzo in his swimwear, especially with a strange little girl in tow. But despite the minor inconvenience, it seemed the proper thing to do.

"Elise?" he said, turning back around to offer his proposal.

To his astonishment, the girl was gone.

He'd had his back to her for but a moment, he thought – not nearly long enough for her to make an exit. Besides, he was quite sure he would have heard the pitter-patter of her tiny feet against the tile. Even within the heated water, a chill fluttered up his spine like a wriggling tadpole.

He scanned the room and its contents, searching for any sign of her behind the pleather upholstered furniture and fancy potted palms. But she was nowhere to be found.

There had to be some rational explanation, Mr. Worthington decided. Maybe he'd simply been lost in thought for far longer than he'd surmised and the girl's grandmother had appeared at the pool's entrance to collect her. His wife had so often accused him of failing to "be present" whenever he set to wandering too long inside his head. And really, that had to be it, he reasoned, as no other scenario made the least amount of sense.

A bit shaken but satisfied that everything had worked itself out somehow, he shrugged off this somewhat unusual encounter and returned his focus to the task at hand.

Deciding upon the breaststroke, he immersed himself completely before pushing off from the wall and letting his body glide beneath the water for the first several meters. As his head broke the surface he began the froglike stroke that would carry him to the pool's opposite end.

With each successive stroke Mr. Worthington came up for air at the start of the motion and then plunged his head below the water as he propelled himself forward during the stroke's second half. It wasn't long before he began to relax, fully engulfed by the near hypnotic movements of his own body.

Each time he rose for a breath, he was afforded a view of the room's far end. It was somewhere around the mid-way point of his 50-meter-long course that he thought he saw something moving down there.

It was subtle and gone in an instant, the way an errant sunbeam might render a well-placed spider's web briefly visible, no more than a swirl within the shadows. But he was almost certain of what he'd seen. His brow furrowed beneath his swimming cap as his head went under.

When he came up again there was nothing there.

Probably just some trick of the light, he thought, nothing to get himself all worked up about. Or maybe it was the girl, Elise, far more proficient at hiding than he'd assumed, and waiting to play a prank upon an unsuspecting old man. He'd *definitely* be having a discussion with her grandmother if that were the case.

He continued on, soon becoming lost once again in the rhythmic movements of his own limbs as he crossed into the deeper end of the pool. So much so that he failed to notice when the chandeliers began to flicker high above.

At just ten meters from the far wall, he came up for air and saw something again. This time it was no flash of movement but a clearly discernible form: the black silhouette of a man standing bathed in the shadows of the room's far corner. The sight was so jarring it caused him to gasp as the forward momentum of his stroke brought him face down into the pool.

He resurfaced sputtering, expelling the sharp tang of chlorinated water from his mouth and throat. He looked once more at where the figure had been and saw nothing. Even still, Elise's words seemed to echo instantly through his mind.

Because that's where the bad man lives.

Treading water, Mr. Worthington tried to wrap his brain around what he'd just witnessed. The rational part of him was already blaming it all on jet lag or his aging vision, but even these simple explanations didn't seem to sit well. Whatever it was that was happening here, he was giving serious thought to cutting short his swim. This place was really starting to get to him.

He nearly turned himself around and swam all the way back to the shallow end, but he was so close to the deep end wall that it seemed foolish not to finish his meager half a lap before calling it quits. Somewhat reluctantly, he resumed his stroke. And with each rise for oxygen, he watched the wall grow closer. When, at last, his hands made contact, something terrible occurred.

The water all around him turned to icy cold. So sudden, in fact, he felt his chest seize up. But as his mind roiled with the panicked thoughts of a possible heart attack, Mr. Worthington looked up to find something far more terrifying standing there above him.

Towering over him was the figure of a man, dark and diaphanous as if fashioned from smoke or from the very shadows themselves. It glared down at him with a pair of coal black eyes that seemed to swim with unspeakable madness. It was hard to make out its other features but it seemed to have a mouth as well, the lips peeled back in a snarl of rage.

Mr. Worthington screamed, his cries echoing back at him from the marble walls.

The figured lunged at him, its arm reaching out, the hand landing upon the top of his swimming cap. And with one powerful motion, it thrust his head below the water.

Arms thrashing, he struggled against it, bubbles of precious oxygen erupting from his mouth. He tried to lock onto the shadow's arm but his frenzied grasping found no purchase. It was as if there was nothing there but the water and the air above it. And yet he could still feel the weight of its hand upon him, its fingers pressed hard into the sides of his skull.

As his eyes bulged beneath the turquoise depths, he watched in horror as the water turned as red as blood around him. Was it his? Was he the one who was bleeding? he scarcely had time to wonder before the shadow pressed him deeper and deeper below the surface, its arm seeming to grow to an impossible length.

He kicked and fought to escape its grip in the crimson liquid now surrounding him but could not break its hold. The shadow's hand had pushed him nearly to the bottom and he could do nothing to stop it. This was the end he could never have imagined.

Soon, his struggles grew faint. His kicking feet slowed to a lazy treading. His limbs went slack. He watched as the last of his oxygen became a flurry of blood red bubbles rising quickly to the surface. Then his lungs began to fill with pool water and the darkness settled in.

* * *

Mrs. Worthington awoke several hours later annoyed to find her husband had yet to return. She leaned over and grabbed her bag from the side of the bed, produced her Cartier and checked the time. *It was only 45 minutes until their reservation!* Chester hadn't come back to wake her and now it would be a small slice of hell to get dressed, do her make-up, catch a cab and make it halfway across town before their table was given away to a more dedicated pair of diners. One simply did not show up late at Il Paradiso.

Somewhat vexed, she rose and went to her luggage. With some expediency and a little luck, she thought she might just be able to pull off an ensemble and a full face in time to get downstairs and have the bellboys hail them a cabbie who wouldn't get them there late. But all that was contingent upon her husband whose whereabouts were currently unknown. Probably still lollygagging about the pool like some silly little boy, she thought.

By the time she had finished dressing, Chester still had not returned. With a slow simmering anger, Mrs. Worthington snatched up her bag and room key, left the suite loudly and rode the elevator down to the lobby.

Behind the enormous marble check-in desk, she found the same attendant who had checked them in was still on duty. A well-pressed young man with a thin mustache whom she had deemed more than a little chatty upon their first encounter.

"*Signora Worthington! Come posso aiutarti?*" he greeted her.

"English, please," Mrs. Worthington said, rolling her eyes.

"But, yes, of course, Signora Worthington. How may I help you?"

"I need you to point me in the direction of your pool. My husband went for a swim, and now we are running late for our reservation."

"Oh, I'm sure your husband would have found that quite impossible, Signora."

"*Impossible?*" Mrs. Worthington said, one eyebrow arching up at him. It was not a word she was used to hearing.

"Oh yes, Signora, our pool here at the Palazzo has not been open for many years. Perhaps Signore Worthington is in the lounge. Or perhaps the spa?"

"Not likely," she said, fixing him with an icy glare. "My husband does not drink before dinner nor waste time in *spas.* And what do you mean the pool has not been open for years?"

"I mean exactly that, Signora. The pool has been drained and locked up for many, many years now."

"And for what reason does a hotel of this supposed caliber not maintain its pool?"

"Well…there were troubles. Troubles with the pool."

"What do you mean troubles?"

The young attendant leaned in closer, adopting a conspiratorial tone. "I maybe shouldn't tell this, Signora, but you see…there was a big story, on the front page even of *Il Messaggero*, back in the '70s. It made quite a big deal out of what happened at the pool. After that, the owners, they decide it's better just to close the pool."

"You've told me absolutely nothing. What happened at the pool?"

The clerk took a quick look over one shoulder, then leaned in closer still. "There was a murder, Signora."

"How ghastly," Mrs. Worthington said, taken aback.

"Yes, and that's not the worst part, Signora."

"And why is that?"

"It was a little girl, Signora. An American girl. The one who was murdered."

"That is positively dreadful. I certainly pray they caught the killer."

"Well, it was bad for the hotel, Signora."

"I can imagine."

"It was especially bad because the man who did it, Signora, he worked here at the hotel at the time. He was...how do you say, sick in the head? Yes?"

"Yes."

"He drowned the girl, and then cut his own throat," the clerk said, dragging his index finger across the front of his neck to illustrate. "They found both of them floating in the pool."

"Well, that's certainly an awful story. Probably one I'd refrain from telling future guests."

"Perhaps, Signora, but some of them actually come for the ghosts."

"What on earth are you talking about?"

"Some people say...the hotel, she is haunted, Signora."

"Hogwash!" Mrs. Worthington said.

And with that, she turned sharply upon her Manolo heels and went to search the grand hotel for her ridiculous husband.

BUTTON, BUTTON

Eryn Hiscock

Hazel heard a knock at her front door one evening, and sure enough, it was one of those community LARPers locals had warned her about. Parched and famished from the rigors of cardboard sword fights, laser duels, and fake combat, they'd drop their phony weapons and ask neighbors if they'd mind feeding and watering them. Hazel had been persuaded to welcome them, even purchasing certain brands of hummus and pita crackers she'd heard they especially liked, just in case.

"It's like that game 'Button-Button'," the locals said. "You never know how many will come, or when, or to whose doorstep."

Tonight at Hazel's door was just one lone role-player wearing a heavily soiled, too-large Confederate soldier's uniform. Hazel recognized the pale blue tweedy fabric with its double row of scuffed brass buttons arranged like a landing strip down the chest from a PBS special she'd once watched on the U.S. Civil War. A fake moustache, curling inward at the edges, clung precariously to the player's upper lip

She laid her musket on Hazel's porch. "Mind if I lay my weapon here?" she asked. Her imitation of a masculine voice was gruff and deep.

"Is it real?"

"Of course it is, madam," she said. "It's wartime. May I come in?"

Hazel opened her door wider and the woman came inside.

"It rained earlier as our troops bellied through the Haverson's cabbage patch with fire cannoning overhead," the player explained, indicating her soiled jacket in fluttering, feminine gestures with hands filthy as if she'd been crawling through mud. "Our enemy's coordinates being roughly the Escobar's chrysanthemums. Now I'm mighty hungry and thirsty, madam. I hate to ask, but – whatever's in your larder – if you'll oblige."

"Larder?" Hazel said.

"Our enemy's retreated to the Soderham's storage shed – just enough time to refuel before their next strike. I'm a crack shot and my fellows need me." She spoke intensely, showering Hazel with a fine mist of spittle per syllable.

"Oh, will they be joining us?" Hazel looked outside. Her porch light illuminated a ten-foot patch with the view beyond all shadow. No one else was out there.

"Maybe later. They might come looking for me."

"Well, I heard you guys like hummus and pitas, so that's what I got – though, I'm pretty sure that wasn't on the menu at any North American deli during the *real* Civil War."

"Whatever you have is perfect, madam."

"Will you be using my property for your games?" Hazel asked. "You know, trespassing?" Hazel only partly teased.

"Oh, no, madam," the soldier said.

"Why?"

"Your property's not fit for battle."

"Why?"

"I'm very hungry, madam," was the only reply Hazel got to that question.

The player saluted Hazel the whole time she was fixing snacks. Hazel knew this because she'd leaned back from her galley kitchen to occasionally check and yep – the silly ham kept it up – even with no one there watching. Hazel plopped hummus into a bowl and arranged some pita crisps on a serving plate. She returned to the foyer with the food and her guest dove in ravenously.

"Wow," Hazel said. "You really *are* hungry. I could make you sandwiches if you like." Why not make the offer? This woman was attacking her plate like a rabid animal.

"That'd be lovely, madam," the player replied between gulping mouthfuls.

"That voice you put on for your games must irritate your throat," Hazel said as she returned from the kitchen to hand over two foil-wrapped peanut butter and banana sandwiches. The player thanked her and tucked them inside her roomy costume. She patted her lips delicately with a napkin, discreetly realigning her moustache as she did so.

"Would you like a lozenge?" Hazel asked.

"No, thank you," the player said.

"Perhaps you should try a different glue for your moustache."

Her guest smoothed her moustache with a crusty hand. "I don't know what you mean."

"Listen – can we be real for a moment here?" Hazel asked. "Are you playing a man because they wouldn't let women fight during the Civil War?" Hazel had been thinking about the motivation behind this character while she was in the kitchen. "That's actually pretty interesting. I mean – I'm sure it happened. Women on the frontlines impersonating—"

"Shh…" the player pressed her index finger to her lips and leaned closer, whispering: "Never say that in the presence of my fellow soldiers. Ever. Please."

"Okay," Hazel said. She hadn't anticipated these guests staying in character. She'd hoped to get to know them as people. Maybe some of the other competitors wouldn't be such method actors as this one. "Please ask your other friends not to drop by tonight," Hazel told her. "It's late and I'm going to bed."

"I'm very sorry, madam," the player said. "I never mean to impose." She peered through a window to the darkness outside. "I'll be going now."

She thanked Hazel with flowery and formal Victorian farewells and elaborate bows, still in full-on hammy actor mode, before saluting her one last time and turning away in one smooth, well-rehearsed pivoting motion on her heel. She marched out the front door, stopping to pick up her musket and sling it over her shoulder. Hazel watched the player's slight silhouette march stiffly away until indiscernible from anything else on the black horizon. It appeared she was so familiar with the terrain that she didn't even need a lantern to guide her through the seemingly bottomless darkness.

* * *

The next morning, Hazel prepared her south garden for planting assorted lettuces and herbs – maybe even some tomatoes. She knew nothing about gardening because she'd lived in the city her whole life and planned to wing it, relying on seeds, water, sunshine and soil.

She knelt at a patch in the far corner and turned the soil, sure it needed airing out – doesn't everything living need airing out sometimes?

Hazel raised her eyes from digging to wipe the trickle of sweat wending toward her ears. She looked through the bordering poplar trees to the sprawling lawns of her new neighbors, the Escobars. Didn't last night's visitor claim she'd trampled their chrysanthemums during their games? The Escobars must *love* that. Hazel planned to drop by later with a casserole or tray of cookies or something – say hello and get their take on things.

Hazel's trowel hit a hard object. She brushed dirt aside before jerking her hand away like she'd touched something red-hot and burning because she'd just unearthed what she was sure was a human jaw with teeth and patches of yellowing skull half-buried in the soil. There were tattered, sun-bleached swatches of the same blue tweedy fabric that role-player from last night had worn. Mud-crusted, tarnished brass buttons from the same uniform were scattered about, as well as a crumpled ball of discarded tinfoil alongside the other peanut butter and banana sandwich Hazel had sent her new friend off with last night, still intact in its smooth foil package and blinking like a beacon in the bright morning sunlight of Hazel's back garden.

WHERE A TOWN ONCE STOOD

C.M. Saunders

Drive out there this afternoon, she said. Get the story, she said. Write it up tonight and have a print-out on my desk by the morning, she said.

Didn't his editor know the place was thirty miles away? It would take Sam at least an hour to drive there and another hour to get back. He wouldn't get home until late afternoon; then he would have to knock out six hundred words or so this evening to hit his deadline. So much for his anticipated early night.

This job on the local rag was supposed to be a dream come true, his route into journalism, maybe eventually landing him a move to one of the national newspapers where there was more money and more prestige.

But it wasn't working out that way.

Like everyone else in the media industry, except the fat cats at the top, who were constantly squeezing budgets then going to meetings forty minutes away via chartered helicopter, he was overworked and underpaid. All the romantic optimism he once harboured about being a famous writer was slowly but surely being sucked out of him.

The newspaper paid so badly they couldn't even attract any worthwhile freelancers, which meant all the writing had to be done in-house by the four-strong editorial team. Occasionally they were supplemented by an intern from the local college, who were still churning out students into an already saturated job market, but those kids were often more trouble than they were worth. That's if they wanted to stay. One boy had recently walked out after less than an hour in the office. Sam couldn't blame him. It was bad enough getting paid to do the job, never mind doing it for free.

Today he was being sent to the little valley village of Tref y Meirw to interview a man who had grown a giant cucumber in his allotment. That was about as exciting as things got on the *Monmouthshire Herald*. A telephone interview wasn't enough for his jobsworth new ed, who maintained it would be easier (what she really meant was cheaper) if Sam took some snaps of the damn thing at the same time, which essentially meant he was doing two people's jobs.

As he wound his way through the narrow country lanes, his progress hampered by having to pull to the side every few minutes to let other cars pass, the grey sky started to spit rain against his windscreen. Fantastic. Bad weather would make the going even slower.

He turned on the wipers and leaned forward in his seat to peer through the glass. The green tree-lined roads, if you could call them that, all looked the same. The satnav told him he was going in the right direction, and he had no option but to have faith in it.

Suddenly, there was a sign. The first one he had seen for ages, apart from the ones telling him to slow down because there was a sharp turn ahead. Sam took his foot off the accelerator so he could read it.

Tref y Meirw   3

He breathed a sigh of relief. Not much farther. Three miles. At least there was less traffic now. These lanes were never meant to be used by cars. When they were first cut out of the countryside, horses and donkeys were the preferred mode of transport.

A few minutes later, the car passed over a cattle grid, and a short time after that the road opened out a little and a sign told him to keep his speed below 30 mph as he was entering a built-up area. It seemed like an unnecessary precaution, as the place was deserted. The high street was typical of hundreds of other high streets scattered all across the Welsh valleys – lots of empty properties and boarded-up windows where small family businesses once prospered, a once-thriving and self-sufficient local community decimated. Most had been driven out of existence by the huge out-of-town supermarket chains where people flocked to get the lower prices. Small private businesses just couldn't compete.

The valleys had been struggling economically ever since they closed so many coal mines after the Miners' Strike in the 1980s, leaving an entire generation out of work and directionless. Sam was just a child then, but he remembered seeing footage of striking miners fighting with police on the picket line. The images had been burned into his brain. The only career options available for the disaffected valley hordes in the twenty-first century lay in minimum wage work in the service sector with very little job satisfaction, even fewer prospects and possibly a zero-hours contract. No, thank you. It was a sad state of affairs that many people were not much better off than they would be claiming benefits, so that was what a lot of them did.

Sam was quite sure the valleys would be completely deserted if people had the means and motivation to leave, or at least somewhere to go. But so few of them did. There was nothing to channel their energy into. Instead, they just festered in these little pockets of civilisation set amongst the once-bountiful green expanses, feeling the bitterness, frustration and resentment build day after day.

He checked his mirrors, indicated, and pulled over to the side of the road outside what appeared to have once been a fish and chip shop. He was looking for Unman street. The satnav told him it was about a hundred metres away, just off the main road. Sam knew how difficult parking and manoeuvring a vehicle around these narrow streets could be, especially if you were unfamiliar with them. He picked up his camera case off the passenger seat, got out of the car, pulled his collar up against the chilly breeze, and set off on foot along the cracked, bubble-gum-decorated pavement.

It was raining more heavily now, and it wasn't long before he began cursing his bad judgement in leaving the vehicle behind. Looking around, he realised the village really was deserted. You could usually find a newsagent or a corner shop open at most times of the day, but not here. He would try to make this a quick job then get the hell out of there, like everyone else had evidently done. He just had to find the guy with the giant cucumber first.

He was certain the satnav had told him to turn left off the main road onto what he presumed would be a residential street. It seemed straightforward enough; the village was so small he couldn't go far wrong. But there was no turning. The left side of the street was a solid block of terraced buildings. Sam's back-up plan, as always, was to use the GPS on his mobile. He reached in his front pocket only to find it empty.

Shit.

He must have left the phone in the car.

Sam quickened his pace. Sooner or later, he'd bump into someone he could ask directions of.

'Fat chance,' he muttered under his breath. Tref y Meirw was a ghost town.

He didn't have time to wander around in the rain all afternoon. He was considering knocking on someone's front door – there were a few ordinary dwellings interspersed among the boarded-up shops – when he noticed something ahead. It looked like an old run-of-the-mill working men's club, but the thing that caught Sam's attention was the light spilling out of the downstairs windows onto the wet pavement outside. As he drew closer, he saw movement inside. A radio or jukebox was playing an old sixties standard, and above the music he swore he could hear the clinking of glasses and the low hum of conversation. It sounded like the place was packed. That would explain why the village was so quiet. Everyone was in the pub. But on a midweek afternoon? Maybe it was a funeral wake or something. Anyway, who was he to judge? If he lived in Tref y Meirw, he'd probably spend all his time in the pub too.

He shuffled up the three steps leading to the front door and pulled it open. The warm air rushed out to greet him, carrying with it the somehow comforting smell of beer. The laughter and chatter was now unmistakable. There was definitely a gathering of some description going on here.

Met with two doors, Sam took the one on the right. To his surprise, it opened into an empty room. Yet he could still hear the din of merrymakers. What the heck?

Then he saw why. The ground floor of the club was split into two separate rooms, with one central bar serving both. This room was empty, but the other was a hive of activity. The bar was staffed by a large, jolly looking man with curly black hair and a red Wales rugby jersey. When Sam entered, the barman was holding court with a small group of what he assumed to be regulars on the opposite side of the bar. When he saw Sam he whirled around, his face breaking into a wide, toothy grin. 'What can I get you?'

Now there was a question. Sam only intended to ask directions, but to do that and leave might be construed as rude. There was also a sense of relief. You could never be sure what kind of reception an outsider would get walking into places like this, but luckily this particular place seemed friendly enough. Besides, now he thought about it, it had been a long morning, a long drive here, and Sam was thirsty. He surveyed the array of labelled taps on the bar until one caught his eye. 'I'll have half a pint of Trooper, please.'

'Just a half?' The jolly barman exaggerated a look of shock and took a step back.

'Yeah, driving,' said Sam by way of explanation.

'Fair enough, no problem.' The barman wiped his hands on a cloth, plucked a glass off a shelf above his head, and started to fill it from an old-fashioned brass pump. 'Anything else?'

'Actually, I wouldn't mind some directions, if you could help me out?'

'Happy to help, boyo. Where're you tryin' to get to?'

'I'm looking for Unman Street. Do you know it?'

'I do, indeed,' the jolly barman replied. 'You're not too far off. Out the door you came in, turn left, go about fifty yards, cross the road and you'll find it on your right.'

'Great, thanks,' said Sam, as he pulled out his notepad and quickly scribbled the directions down so he wouldn't forget.

'Not from around 'ere, then?'

'Er, no. I'm a journalist. I work for the *Monmouthshire Herald*.' Despite himself, Sam couldn't help but feel his chest flush with pride whenever he told anyone what he did for a living.

'Writer, eh?'

'Yes, doing a piece about the guy who grew a giant cucumber.'

This made the barman chuckle. 'Is that right? Can't think who that could be. Takes all sorts, I s'pose. Anything else?'

Sam suddenly found the journalist in him rising to the fore. 'I was just wondering why this place is so full on a weekday afternoon? Is it a private party?'

The barman chuckled again. 'Private party? Nope, day

shift crew, innit? Come in 'ere most days for a pint after work, see?'

'Day shift crew? From a factory?'

The barman looked at Sam as if he had just grown a second head. 'Factory? It's the pit, innit? Miners. Black gold seekers.'

'Miners? But I thought the pits were all closed.'

'Not likely. Enjoy the Trooper,' the barman said as he put a glass down in front of Sam and went off to serve another customer.

Sam took his drink and took a seat at an empty table in the corner, from where he could see the bar and the other room. True enough, every one of the patrons were working-age males, and even from this distance, he could make out the tell-tale blue scars of a career spent underground. His maternal grandfather had worn the same wounds like badges of honour. When Sam was a child, he remembered thinking someone had been drawing on his granddad with a pen and spent hours trying to rub off the 'ink'. Only later did he find out that the network of deep blue scars carved into his granite flesh were the result of a life spent on the coalfaces. Coal dust worked its way into the cuts and grazes, and when they healed, left blue scars.

Sam listened to the ebb and flow of conversation and the frequent outbursts of laughter, occasionally stealing a glance over. If what the jolly barman said was right and this was habitual, it showed in the men's manner. Everyone was in high spirits. The banter was good-natured and there were always people waiting to be served at the bar. When someone bought a drink they never bought just one; they always seemed to be buying a round. Mostly pints of beer and ale, with the occasional whisky or brandy chaser. It was a sign of community spirit sadly lacking in most places.

And there was something else. Some, if not most, of the men were smoking. Smoking indoors in this day and age! Sam supposed as long as nobody complained, the jolly landlord would just let them carry on. It was either that or reprimand them and risk them taking their apparently considerable business elsewhere. It wasn't exactly socially acceptable anymore, but Sam sure as hell wasn't going to walk into a room full of tough-as-nails coal miners and tell them all to stub their fags out. He wouldn't last two minutes.

Whatever. The cold beer tasted just as it should. Malty and somehow earthy, not like the masses of commercial lagers stuffed full of additives and preservatives that flooded high street pubs in the cities. You could always count on small local pubs for a good pint. Or half a pint, whatever the case may be.

All too soon, however, Sam's glass was empty. He toyed with the idea of getting another. He could get another half, or even two, and, he reasoned, still be under the legal drink drive limit. But he knew from experience that it was much easier to walk out of a pub after one drink than it was after two. Besides, he was technically at work. He took his glass back to the bar, caught a wink of gratitude from the jolly barman, and left through the same door he went in.

It had stopped raining now, which was something at least, but the wind had picked up and it was already beginning to get dark. Swings and roundabouts. Sam pulled out his notebook where he had scribbled the directions the barman had told him.

Out the door you came in, turn left, go about fifty yards, cross the road and you'll find it on your right.

He followed the directions to the letter, and moments later found himself standing in Unman Street, outside the address he was looking for. He knocked the door and waited. No answer. He knocked again as a small part of him wilted. 'Oh God, please don't let this be a wasted journey.'

It was a mid-terrace house. Small, and typical of houses in the coalfields. Most villages were made up of two distinct types: a row or two of larger three-bedroom dwellings for the colliery management, and dozens of small two-bedroom dwellings like this for the miners and their families. Sam took a few steps back and looked up. There were no lights on, neither upstairs nor down. But that was no real indicator; despite the waning light, it was that time of day that didn't really require artificial lighting. Especially if the homeowners were skimping on electricity, which, of course, most homeowners were.

He considered knocking on a neighbour's door, then decided against it. How could they possibly help the situation? 'Oh, giant cucumber man? Yes, he lives next door. He's out, you say? Well, isn't that your hard luck?'

Instead, he made up his mind to get out of Tref y Meirw and make his way home. He had a contact number for the cucumber man. He would get him on the phone tomorrow and ask him to send through some digital images of his handiwork. In Sam's experience, people of that disposition took a lot of photos hoping that some day someone would ask to see them. The article wouldn't be as good as it could have been, and it would be on the editor's desk half a day late, but what was he supposed to do?

At the office the next morning, Sam couldn't stop thinking about his visit to Tref y Meirw, and in particular the working men's club. For some reason, it stuck in his head. He googled it, hoping the club may have a website or a Twitter account he could follow. Failing that, maybe he could leave a nice review on TripAdviser.

The first page brought no hits. Ditto the second. The village was mentioned, but not the working men's club. The third page yielded the same result.

What the hell?

Then, as he scrolled through yet more Google pages, Sam stumbled upon a headline on an archived news site, dated 27th March 1983.

ELEVEN DEAD IN PUB TRAGEDY

Ten patrons, along with the landlord, Cyril Williams, 44, died yesterday when fire suddenly swept through the Meirw Working Men's Club in the village of Tref y Meirw. All the dead are believed to have been trapped in a back room where they had been drinking after hours. An investigation is ongoing, and the cause of the blaze is unknown. Foul play is not suspected.

There was a faded black-and-white picture accompanying the article, clearly showing the place Sam had been drinking in not twenty-four hours earlier. In front of the building stood the jolly landlord.

THE LAST RIDE

Angelique Fawns

Sabrina stared up at the abandoned Ferris wheel. It loomed forgotten on a run-down section of Myrtle Beach. It was impossible to tell what colours may have once decorated the swings sitting on the rusty frame. Dust and decay coating any memory of the laughing passengers of years ago. The crowds had migrated to the modern SkyWheel located on the popular Oceanfront Broadwalk and Promenade. It had a completely different feel to it. A metallic monstrosity which carried passengers in gondolas and soared an unbelievable height into the clouds.

Sabrina didn't like riding the SkyWheel. Being in a small enclosed space made her feel claustrophobic. Just one of the many phobias she dealt with on a daily basis. In fact, there was nothing she liked about the popular tourist area. The crowds made her feel panicky. At seventeen years old, she could be the poster child for mental health issues. Even now in March, after the school break crowds had gone back to class, it was still sensory overload. Cars blared music and cruised the main drag until all hours of the morning, some even with the modified shocks that made them jump up and down. Mothers hollered at over-sugared kids tearing up and down the beach.

A cool wind was blowing off the ocean tonight, making the open-air chairs rock and creak. This area was one of her favorite places to walk in the evening. There was something soothing about the boarded-up vacation cottages and decrepit boardwalks deemed not worth fixing after the last hurricane. They were damaged. She was damaged. Her ponytail had loosened and the strands were blowing into her eyes and face. Pulling the band off, she tried to tuck her hair back into its tight configuration. It took her three tries. Everything took her three tries. Every light switch had to be flipped three times. Her shoelaces tied three times. When she was typing her schoolwork, she read over every paragraph precisely three times.

Her peculiarities really didn't start to manifest until puberty hit. As a child, they just thought she was quiet and shy. Then as a tween she became plagued with panic attacks and obsessive-compulsive behaviour. Her parents hauled her to doctors and psychologists. The diagnosis was mild Asperger's syndrome, something they had missed when she was younger. She zoned out in the office when the doctor was explaining everything, so Sabrina googled it later. Basically, you have normal intelligence and language, but impairment with social skills and prone to repetitive or restricted behaviour. Yup, that was her in a nutshell. She did go to therapy once a week to work on her communication and develop coping techniques, but honestly, it felt like a waste of time.

How could she explain why she had to do almost everything in a multiple of three? She tried to give her mother and friends a physics lesson. How three was nature's favourite number. That there are three types of stable neutrons: The proton, the neutron, and the electron. And how all solid matter is made of atoms built entirely from these three particles. Science explained her OCD perfectly – one good thing she got out of high school. Everyone else was missing the logic. So she checked the lock three times after shutting the door. Brushed her teeth for exactly six minutes. Thirty-three strokes of her hair every night.

Of course, she got teased at school because of it, or just ignored. There were a few kids who tolerated her, and she even had one close friend who found her quirky and fun. Dierdre started hanging out with her in seventh grade, and never minded waiting while Sabrina zipped and unzipped her coat three times. Now they were both in grade eleven, and Dierdre's social life had blossomed while Sabrina became even more introverted. She had been invited out tonight with Deirdre and a few others to go to Applebee's for snacks. Sabrina felt ill thinking about the Friday night crowds at the chain restaurants. Plus, she hated watching the other girls roll their eyes when Sabrina started removing the ice cubes from her Sprite until there were exactly three cubes (or six or nine) in her glass.

Instead she was here, alone, staring up at a depressing amusement ride. She lied to her parents and told them that she was joining Dierdre for the girl's night out. Her folks were relieved whenever she put down a historical romance novel (her favourite escape) and went out like a normal teen. Her curfew was a reasonable 11:00pm, so that gave her plenty of time to stride the deserted streets finding relief in the fresh air and solitude.

She was about to start her loop back home, when the Ferris wheel creaked and started to slowly rotate.

"What! Is anybody there? Is this a trick?"

Peering through the gloom, she couldn't see anyone at the base of the old amusement ride. In fact, there was a chain-link fence around the perimeter to discourage playing or climbing on it. The terrible creaking sound tore at her eardrums.

"Hello? Is anyone over there? This isn't a good joke!"

No one answered. Sabrina took a closer look at the chain-link and found that someone had pulled up a section just big enough for a small person to crawl through. Dropping to her knees, she slithered through the opening, swearing when a bit caught and tore her jacket. The Ferris wheel was picking up speed, and she could hear soft music.

Getting closer, she noticed the Ferris wheel wasn't as decrepit as she first thought. The music got louder, a fun jazzy piece. Then laughter and chatting. Sabrina closed her eyes and gave her head a shake to clear her ears.

When she opened her eyes, things REALLY didn't make sense. The sun was shining, people were milling everywhere and a five-piece band was rocking out under a big white gazebo. It was like a scene from one of her historical romance novels. The Ferris wheel was shiny with fresh paint and every seat was full. Ladies in frilly dresses, fascinators, and parasols sat delicately as they were whisked around and around. Kids laughed beside them, while men kept one arm around their dates and another on their hats.

Sabrina stood there with her mouth open. What was this? Had she slipped, hit her head, and was now lying in the dirt? Taking her hand, she pinched her arm, three times, hard. Yes, it hurt and yes, she was still standing in a world that had transformed itself into a lively and lovely day at an old-time fair. How many times had she read her novels and wished she could be whisked into the pages?

"Ma'am step right up! We have a seat for you right here," a young man in a colourful suit called to her.

The Ferris wheel slowed down and an empty chair stopped at the bottom. Sabrina hurried up the steps to the platform and took the young man's proffered hand. If she was dreaming, she might as well enjoy a ride. He helped her settle into an empty car, and shut the safety bar tightly.

"Enjoy the view, ma'am, and have a lovely day! We hope you stay a while," he said with a big grin and a quick bow.

The Ferris wheel started back up again, and it was glorious. The sun was warm, and the view was spectacular. There were no garish signs advertising tourist attractions, no big freeways, just trees and perfect little houses with the ocean glistening nearby. A small boy in the car in front of her turned backwards and waved at her enthusiastically. Sabrina felt happy.

After several rotations, the Ferris wheel slowed, stopped, and Sabrina's car rocked gently at the top of the structure. Must be time to load on new passengers.

A woman in the chair behind her shouted, "You can stay here forever if you want!"

Sabrina turned and saw a lovely young lady in a yellow frilly dress and matching feather hat.

"You can live here with us and ride the Ferris wheel whenever you want!" the yellow lady said.

"How can I do that?" Sabrina asked, feeling excited. She didn't want the ride to end.

"You just have to jump," said a man in a dapper blue suit from the front car. He must be the child's father.

"What? How does that make any sense?" Sabrina asked.

"You can stay here forever. We have fun everyday!" his son said, bouncing on his knees in the seat.

"Yes, stay with us Sabrina, join us Sabrina, we want you Sabrina…" all the riders on the Ferris wheel started to chant.

The sound of their voices and the rocking of the Ferris wheel in the breeze seemed almost hypnotic. What would she be going home to? A life where she was lonely? Where she never fitted in?

"Just jump, Sabrina, and you can have fun forever in this wonderful world," the yellow-dress lady said.

Yes, she could stay here forever. Like living in one of her books. She started pushing up the safety latch.

The voices got more excited as the sounds of the band faded. "Yes Sabrina, join us Sabrina, jump Sabrina…"

She raised the safety bar up once and brought it back down again. Then she did it for a second time.

"Hurry Sabrina, we are so hungry Sabrina…"

Her hand paused as she heard the voices chanting. Hungry? She looked away from the latch toward the lady in the yellow dress. Except this time her dress was ripped and black. And her face was no longer peach perfect with rosy cheeks. Bones peeked out from decayed flesh. The little boy was grey with teeth missing and one eye lolling out of its socket. Clouds had passed in front of the sun and shadows darkened the fair.

Sabrina gasped and shoved away from the safety bar. She had been just starting her third unlocking of the latch. The final unlatching.

"Damn. Too greedy." The ghoul turned back into a pretty lady and smiled at her. The music swelled again and the clouds passed on. "Come on Sabrina, you will love living with us!"

Sabrina pushed her body back against the seat and took a tight grip of the bars. She couldn't believe how close she had come to jumping. Would she have been committing suicide? Keeping her eyes screwed tight, she counted to twelve. When she opened her eyes, it was night again, and she was sitting in a rusted old car swinging at the top of the Ferris wheel. The people, the music, and the old town were gone.

All she could hear was the whistling of the wind and the distant roar of the interstate, but no brassy band. How had the Ferris wheel moved? If she wasn't a hundred feet in the air, she could have told herself she imagined the whole thing. She didn't have her cell phone on her. She'd wanted solitude so had come out without it, as for sure Deirdre would be calling her, telling her to come join the crowd. So, she couldn't phone anyone for help. There was no one on the streets to call to, and she definitely didn't want to spend another minute on this haunted contraption. Looking down, she saw that there was a complicated configuration of bars and struts holding the ride together. It looked climbable. Taking a deep breath, she crawled out of the car and slowly made her way down.

Were those hands plucking at her T-shirt? The metal was cold and rough under her palms, but she hung on tightly and scrambled down. A few little cuts started bleeding on her palms where stiff peeling paint and rough metal nicked them.

She thought she could hear a whispering in her ear, "Jump Sabrina, let go Sabrina, it would be so easy…"

Distracting herself, she envisioned the atoms of the Ferris wheel in groups of three and muttered to herself, "We have three atoms, which become six, which become nine, which become twelve…"

She still imagined cold hands and voices, but she could become completely distracted when she counted atoms. Grunting and concentrating, she made her way down to the ground. As soon as her feet hit the dirt, she scrambled back under the fence and turned around to look back. The antique cars swung slowly and hypnotically in the breeze, but they weren't rotating. Shuddering, she swore to herself that was the very last time she would ever ride a Ferris wheel. As she started walking away there was a whisper in the breeze.

"Come back Sabrina… we will be waiting…"

THE WALKING WOMAN

Christopher Wilson

August 27, 2007

It was the sound of raucous laughter that startled the birds from their hiding spots, as it rolled and bounced amongst the trees and seemed to have the power to hold back the coming twilight. The kind of laughter that is born in the untroubled freedoms of teenage boys.

"There is no way you just did that," laughed Jim.

John Doris was around the back of the old burgundy Windstar. He was doubled over, both hands resting on his knees, as his friends, Jim Brown, Dave Wilson, and Colin Mills, stood around watching in disbelief. John's face was already bright red, thick perspiration forming on his brow as he chewed furiously to get the third habanero pepper down.

"Done!" John stood up and opened his mouth wide, twisting his head from side to side so that all the boys could see.

"I told you there was nothing that Johnny couldn't eat," explained Colin.

John grinned wide, tears still streaming down his face. "Now I want the five bucks you owe me so that I can get something to wash this down."

"Yeah, yeah, yeah," said Jim as he fished into his pocket for the last of his summer money, then watched as John ran into Jay Bird's Gas & Variety to spend his winnings.

That's how it had been while Jim stayed with his mom for the summer. The four friends engaged in an endless game of one-upmanship. It was their way to fight off the boredom that comes from living in a small central-Ontario town.

"I'm sure you'll get a chance to win it back," said Colin. He patted Jim on the shoulder and then went to sit on the bumper of the van.

"He's taken a lot of money from me this summer."

"How much?" asked Colin.

"Close to two hundred bucks," Jim sighed. "I need to come up with a way to get it back."

John returned, handing each of the boys a cold drink. "What's gotcha down, blue eyes?" he asked Jim.

Colin snorted, amused at the poke. "He wants to win his money back."

"I see," John mused. "And how do you propose to do that?"

"That my friend," Dave interjected, "is the million dollar question."

Dave chugged the last of his cola and crushed the can, absentmindedly tossing it into the back of the van.

"What if he walked *the road*?" John asked.

"No," Dave quickly responded.

"Why not?" asked John.

"Yeah, why not?" echoed Colin.

"Which road?" interrupted Jim.

"Old Pit Road," answered John.

"Old Pit Road?"

"Concession Road 3," clarified Colin.

"Okay, so Concession Road 3, what about it?" asked Jim.

"It's because you're not from around here," answered Dave, wearing a look of concern on his face.

"He doesn't have to do it, Dave. It was just an idea," said John.

"Guys—" started Jim.

"No, it's a great idea," interrupted Colin, jumping up from his seat on the bumper. "He did say he wanted to win his money back."

"It would be big," agreed John.

"Yeah, but I just don't think it's a good idea," said Dave.

"Guys!" Jim interrupted, bringing the argument to a halt.

"What?" asked Colin.

"What's the big deal with Old Pit Road?"

A look flashed between John, Dave, and Colin. "There was a local woman who was killed around twenty years ago – well that's where it happened," explained John.

"That's not the whole story." Dave glared at John.

"Well, what is?" asked Jim.

"Her name was Rose Chambers, and she wasn't killed – she was murdered," stated Dave.

"So what happened?"

"Rose Chambers disappeared while hiking in McCreary park. She'd gone out early in the morning and when she hadn't returned by the evening her parents said they had known something was wrong. The police found her car in the visitors' lot where she'd left it, and shortly after began a search of the area. I think it was around day three or four when they found one of her shoes and her backpack. There was no other sign of what happened to her."

Dave paused and rubbed the back of his neck. "What happened to her was that she'd run into Kurt Hill. He followed her into the park and stalked her on the hiking trail. He jumped her when she stopped for lunch, and overpowered her. He bound her and took her to an old hunting cabin close to Old Pit Road. He kept her prisoner there for several days, torturing her and doing... *other* things to her. Finally, he'd gotten bored with her and decided that he was ready to move on. But Hill was a sick *sonofabitch,* so he stripped her naked and then close to twilight, forced her at gunpoint to trek through the woods. She was already so maimed from the torture that it was nearly impossible to walk. Hill forced her on her hands and knees to crawl through the woods, up the steep embankment, where she collapsed onto Old Pit Road.

"He explained to her that Old Pit ran east for another two and a half kilometres, before it crossed the next concession road. Hill, the sadistic fuck, then made her his final offer. She was to get up and start walking east on the road and if anyone were to drive by and was willing to help her, he would let her go. If, however, she made it to the concession road without being picked up, he was going to kill her. He also told her that he would be in the woods off to the side of the road, following, and if she stopped walking or left the road for any reason, he would kill her. She would know he was there, he told her, because she would be able to see the light of his electric lantern. She begged him to let her go, and pleaded with him not to kill her. Her only chance, he taunted, was to be rescued on the course of her walk, and to emphasize the painful alternative, he cut off one of her fingers."

Dave paused and took a big breath. "You know how this story ends. She was found the next day where Old Pit Road meets Concession Road 6. Her naked body was in the middle of the road, stabbed eight times in the belly, laying in a pool of her dried blood."

Jim stood in silence for a few moments considering what he'd just heard. "Like hell that's a real story."

"What do you mean?" asked Dave.

"Well, if she was dead when they found her, then how do you know any of the details of her final days, other than cause of death?"

"I'd have thought that was obvious," said Dave.

"How?"

"They caught Kurt Hill," added John.

"The police caught him a few days after he killed Rose," continued Dave.

"And what, he just told the police that he killed her?"

"Kurt Hill was bat shit crazy," explained Dave, "and he pretty much told the police everything right down to the last detail. He practically bragged about how he pelted her with rocks to keep her moving along the road. He even confessed to several other brutal crimes, and the police were able to confirm that he was wanted in BC, and several U.S. states. My mom told me that in the end he was extradited to Texas. He was sentenced to death, and finally executed. That guy was a psycho who wanted to be famous."

"Okay, it's a terrible story," Jim agreed, "but what does it have to do with walking the road?"

"Well, it wasn't long afterward that strange things began to happen on that part of the road."

"Like what?" asked Jim, who felt more than ever, he was being drawn into one of those *friend of a friend* stories that end with death by Pop Rocks and Coca-Cola.

"Well, for one, all of the trees died at the trail marker, the area where Hill forced Rose out of the woods," explained Dave.

"Dead trees? Is that the best you can do?"

"No," objected Dave, "there are other things."

"People have reported seeing strange lights moving around in the trees," added John.

"People driving through at night have said that when they see the lights their cars are sometimes hit with rocks," Colin chimed in.

"And," Dave continued, "the OPP[1] have responded to reports of a woman walking down the road who appears to be in distress."

"So the road is haunted?"

"Basically," finished Dave.

"They say that she's looking for someone to finally help her," added John.

"Who's they?"

"You know," Colin jumped in, "us locals."

---

[1] Ontario Provincial Police

That was enough for Jim. It fired in him a need to make these local boys pay through the nose. "What would I have to do?"

"Well," said John, "starting at Concession Road 4 you'll have to walk east on Old Pit Road until you come to Concession Road 6."

"How long does it take to walk that distance?"

"Twenty-five minutes, maybe thirty, if you're slow," said John.

"That's it?"

"That's it," confirmed John.

Jim stood for a moment, thinking he'd heard some genuine concern in Dave's voice; however, he really did want to end the summer on a high note. "I'll do it, but I want to raise the stakes. If I'm successful, I want all of my money back from John, plus another twenty-five bucks each from you two. If I lose, John, you of course keep the money, plus I'll throw in another twenty-five for each of you."

"Done," agreed John.

"I'm in," said Colin.

The three of them stood there looking at Dave. He was uncomfortable with the situation, but with nothing more than a gut feeling that it might not be the best idea, he could think of no other reason to object to the bet. "Alright, I'm in for the twenty-five."

"Okay, so how do we do this?" asked Jim.

John already had a plan. "We'll all drive out to Concession 4 and Old Pit, you'll get out, and we'll drive to Concession 6 and wait for you there."

"No good."

"Why not?" asked Colin.

"How do I know one of you jackasses won't get out of the van once you are out of sight and then do your best to scare me from the trees?"

"Tell you what," said Dave offering a solution, "we'll drop you off at Concession 4 and Old Pit and then we'll backtrack to town and drive east across Main and then back up Concession 6 to Old Pit. That way you won't have to worry about us trying anything funny."

"When should we do this?"

"I was thinking now," suggested John.

"Tonight might be ideal," confirmed Dave. "It's nice and warm and the moon is nearly full, so there will be lots of light for you to see by."

"Okay then, let's get going," exclaimed John.

A few minutes later the burgundy Windstar pulled out of the parking lot of Jay Bird's Gas & Variety and sped north out of town toward Old Pit Road. The moon was high in the sky, reflecting ethereal light over the landscape.

* * *

The van was parked on the shoulder of the dark road. It was a perfect summer night, the warm night air was inviting to the skin, and the aromatic scent of pine hung thick in the air. Jim stood in the intersection staring down Old Pit Road. It was an old service road, carved through the thick woods and laid down while the quarry was still in operation. Under the moonlight the darkness could do little to hide the wear in the road, the once smooth blacktop now marred with cracks and potholes.

"About twenty-five minutes to Concession 6, right?" asked Jim without taking his eyes off the road before him.

"Yup," answered Dave, leaning out of the passenger side window.

The side door opened and John hopped out. "Take this," he said, handing Jim a small plastic flashlight. "You sure you want to do this?"

Jim switched the flashlight on and off a couple of times, making sure it would work. Satisfied, he stuffed it into his pocket. "Yeah, but let's get started before I change my mind."

John climbed back into the van and pulled the side door shut. The gravel on the shoulder popped and cracked as the van slowly rolled forward and pulled a tight U-turn to get pointed back toward town. Coasting to a slow stop in the intersection, Colin lowered the driver side window.

"Listen, if you can't do it, just follow this road back to town and make your way to the Jay Bird," explained Colin. "We'll give you forty minutes to make Concession 6 before we start to drive this way on Old Pit."

"Sounds good."

"Good luck," Dave shouted from inside the van.

Colin gave it some gas and the van sped off down the road. Jim stood and watched the taillights until they finally disappeared in the distance, leaving him alone in the intersection.

Jim started down Old Pit, slowly at first, but once he realized that a ghostly lady wasn't going to jump out at him from the trees, he picked up the pace. He felt foolish. He couldn't believe that he had let them get to him with their ghost story. It was a great story for sure, but it wasn't going to keep him from winning this bet.

The road bent sharply to the right and then straightened out as it dipped into a shallow plain. The tall pines pushed right up to the shoulders of the road leaving Jim feeling a little boxed in. He chuckled to himself as he realized that he was walking down the center of the road, following the dividing line like Hansel and Gretel's trail of breadcrumbs.

The road began to rise, bringing itself out of the natural depression. As it crested, Jim noticed a sign to his left, the trail marker, reflected in the moonlight. It brought him to a halt. The general peacefulness of his night walk drained away as the story of Rose Chambers came back to him.

"What was it that Dave said?" he asked himself. "The trees died at the trail marker."

Such was the illumination provided by the moon that Jim could easily see that the pines clustered around the marker had withered and died, standing now only as skeletal monuments. Fishing the flashlight from his pocket, Jim switched it on and cast a cone of light on the area. He noticed a large crack in the shoulder of the road that began at the base of the sign. He traced the crack with his light and saw that it ran from the base of the sign, across the shoulder and then split the road from one side to the other.

Jim took a few more steps forward and then stopped again at the crack in the road. He hesitated to cross this Rubicon. A bit of childhood wisdom came to mind. "Step on a crack, break your mother's back," he said to the moon. He held his breath as he took one big exaggerated step over the break in the road. When nothing happened, he exhaled.

"Alright, let's get this done." He turned his eyes back to the road and pressed on.

He started a silent count of his paces, thinking he might be able to approximate his walking speed. He hadn't gone far, about seventy paces, when a crack from somewhere behind him brought him to a stop. It was the sound of snapping branches. He waited for more noise, but there was none. He turned and looked back from where he came. Though the moon was high in the sky, its illumination seemed choked out by the corridor of tall pines, and he could hardly make out the trail marker, despite its reflective paint. And there was something else. It looked to Jim as if there was a large black something on the road just out of reach of the sign. Was it moving? No? He strained and squinted his eyes trying to make out what he was seeing, but it did no good. If he wanted to know what it was, he would simply have to go back. Even out here on this lonely road, the pull of his natural curiosity was strong. It was the practical part of him that interceded and reminded him that he had over two hundred bucks riding on this walk, and that time was of the essence.

Yet he stood there on the road, the first faint fingers of vapour curling around his lips from the cooling night air, until he could provide an explanation to himself of what he was seeing. It was the condition of the road that held the answer. All he was seeing was a shadow caused by a depression in the road made visible now by his relative position. He rubbed his arms for a little warmth. "Okay, now I'm just getting myself worked up. Get a move on, Jim." Again, he turned and forced himself to resume his walk.

The road bent to the right and before too long the trail marker and the black spot were out of sight. He focused on the road, and tried once again, to come up with a reasonable guess as to how fast he was travelling. How long had he been on the road? Fifteen minutes? Longer? It was hard to tell. Certainly, his friends would now be at the meeting point. It would be a relief to be off this road and in the van.

From the darkness, an unearthly wail arose to pierce the night air, causing his blood to freeze and his body to become rigid. "Holy shit!" He was afraid to move. The hairs on his arms and neck stood up as a shiver passed through him. Watching wisps of his breath escape into the darkness, it was the first time he realized just how cold the night had become. He twisted quickly to look back down the road. Off in the distance, just beyond the shoulder of the road, a few paces into the tangle of pines he could see a soft blue light moving through the darkened woods. It moved slowly following the line of the road. What was it? An orb that was much too big to be a firefly and at times seemed to flicker like a flame. Whatever it was, it was making its way toward him. Would it simply pass him by? Jim was sure he didn't want to wait to find out. He was about to turn when he saw something else. He had been so distracted by the blue light that he hadn't noticed that there was something on the road. It too was hard to make out against the blackness of the road, but whatever it was it carried itself fairly low to the ground. Was it a large dog? Something moving on four legs? Jim strained to see it, its slow and jerky movements just enough to keep it ahead of the flickering light. It was his need to know that reminded him he had a flashlight in his pocket. Pulling it out, he levelled it at the black mass moving down the road. He shivered as his thumb fingered the switch. He simply had to turn it on to solve this mystery. As he stood there on that lonely patch of Old Pit Road he knew he already had the answer. The only thing light would do is remove the uncertainty of the situation. Better to not know. Better to run.

Jim stuffed the flashlight back into his pocket, turned and broke into a run. Furiously pumping his fists, he ran as if the devil were at his heels. Again, from behind, came a wail which chilled him to the bone, a wail that was so utterly devoid of hope that it pained him to the heart, as there could be no doubt it was born of the cruellest suffering. It drove him forward and he ran until his lungs burned. The cracked road was hard under his feet, but still he ran and dared not look back.

There was a loud crack from the woods to his left as something unseen forced its way through the trees that surrounded the road. A stinging pain, small and sudden, on his cheek just below his left eye, startled him. Had he run into something? No. Even as he wheezed, he realized he had been struck. A small rock skipped off the toe of his shoe. Flung from the woods, rocks continued to strike both him and the road around him. They made sharp cracks as they hit the blacktop, hurled at him with increasing intensity each time. He pushed himself on, step after step on the pitted road, attempting a running zigzag to avoid being hit. A rock ricocheted off his ankle causing him to stumble. Arms flailing, he took five or six wildly out of control steps before he managed to slow and regain his balance. He had just a moment of relief before he was struck on the side of the head by a rock the size of a walnut. His knees buckled and he stumbled backward, his vision blurring before he toppled onto the road.

He fought to stay conscious as he lay there on the road looking up into the starry sky. It was the sensation of warm blood seeping out of his wound and running into his hair which ultimately kept him in the here and now. Faintly at first, he became aware of a sound on the road. It was erratic and halting, the unmistakable sound of bare feet slapping on the blacktop. The hair on his arms and the back of his neck stood up. He could feel the air around him getting cold, his breath condensing in the air. He rolled over onto his belly so that he could look back down the road.

There she was, Rose Chambers, shuffling toward him. She was naked, extremely pale, and despite the darkness and distance, Jim could see that her body was marred from head to toe with deep cuts, angry welts, and ugly black bruises. The flesh on her knees had been scraped away during her crawl through the forest, leaving them crusted over with blood and dirt. There was blood, thick and black, dried on her inner thigh, further evidence of her savage treatment. Her belly was punctured with eight wicked wounds, now black and crusty. Most horrible was her face, contorted from her suffering into something only vaguely human. Her cracked and blackened lips parted and a moan gurgled up from her throat, like a banshee, causing any of his remaining courage to fail. Paralyzed with fear, he could only watch as the walking nightmare closed the distance, one halting step at a time. Jim began to scream.

It was the sound of his own screaming that finally

broke the spell. She was close, maybe too close, but Jim scrambled to his feet to make his getaway. As he rose, she grabbed at him, her gnarled hand with its missing finger clutching at his shoulders. Jim struggled, but she pulled him close and opened her mouth as if to speak. He thrust his hand up into her face, catching her under the chin, forcing her mouth closed; the skin of her face and chin was cold, and cracked against the palm of his hand. He shoved his other hand into her chest and pushed against her with all of his might. With a cry, he pushed until he broke her grip. She staggered back, but caught his extended hand, pulling him to the ground with her as she fell backward.

He came down hard on her twisted legs and there was a sickening crunch as bone and flesh were ground into the blacktop. There was no sound from her, no indication that she felt anything at all. Her body was cold as the grave, and it was unbearable to be pressed against it. Jim struggled to free himself from the entanglement, but she was already grabbing at his head and shoulders. He continued to strike at her face and arms, breaking any hold that she was able to get, and worked himself to his knees. He rained his fists down upon the corpse, a flurry of blows that pushed back her assault. Finally on his feet, he turned to run, but as he stepped she grabbed his ankle with both hands, sending him crashing into the road, his face and nose taking the brunt of the impact. It was his last attempt at escape.

Whatever this Rose was, she pulled herself up and along Jim's legs, hand over hand, getting closer to his head. The cold from her body was smothering and numbing, and sapped all of Jim's strength. Like some kind of ghoulish constrictor, she engulfed his body with her own, until at last he was at the end. Even as she leaned in close, he was aware of his screaming. Her bloodied and cracked lips parted and the last thing he heard, cutting through his screams, was the icy, dead voice of Rose Chambers in his ear, "*not alone.*"

July 8, 2019

It was the sound of raucous laughter that startled the birds from their hiding spots. It rolled and bounced amongst the trees, and seemed to have just enough power to hold back the coming twilight for a little while longer. It was the kind of laughter that is born in the untroubled freedoms of teenage girls.

"There is no way you actually did that," laughed Jill.

"Well, it's true. He'd been harassing me for months, so I forwarded the whole lot of them to his mom," Alexandra said with a grin, "and voila, I haven't heard from Steve since."

"I told you she did it," said Emma, and the three girls once again burst into laughter.

When she'd finally caught her breath, Jill rolled down the window to let some of the warm summer air into her car. "What do you want to do tonight?"

"Tonight is a perfect night for a bonfire and some ghost stories," said Emma, "and we can call Jeff, Dave, and Mike to see if they will join us. You can always count on those guys to bring beer."

"No, let's do something really scary. Let's walk the road," countered Jill.

"Walk the road?" asked Alexandra.

"Yeah," agreed Emma, "let's walk the road."

"What does that mean?"

"It means that if we go out to Old Pit Road we might be able to see some weird shit," said Emma.

"Yeah, Old Pit is haunted," added Jill.

"Oh sure, a lot of people around here have seen strange lights, sounds, and more," said Emma.

"More? A ghost?" asked Alexandra.

Emma and Jill exchanged glances, a silent confirmation of local connection, and of a whispered horror seldom shared with outsiders.

"Yeah, we might see the ghost of a woman," said Emma.

The three girls sat in the car in silence considering what was before them, and it was a few moments before Jill spoke up. "We might also see the boy."

ELEANOR

C.E. Rickard

'Ruby, come on inside now. Dinner is ready,' Erin called from inside the kitchen doorway. She leaned against the doorframe and smiled as she watched her daughter skipping around the apple tree near the end of the garden.

'Woo hoo, I'm starving,' Ruby squealed as she ran up the garden towards the house. 'Can Eleanor stay for dinner too, pleeease?'

'Who is Eleanor?' Erin asked, holding the door open as Ruby skipped past her with a giggle. 'Ruby, I said, who is…oh never mind,' she laughed and followed her daughter into the room. She placed two bowls of hot soup onto the small, round table and sat down next to Ruby.

'No!' Ruby shouted. 'Eleanor is sitting there.'

'Hey, don't shout,' Erin answered, startled 'You made me jump.'

'Move Mummy. Eleanor is sitting there!' Ruby replied, tears glinting in the corners of her eyes.

'Okay, okay. I'll move.' Erin got to her feet and shifted round to the next chair. 'But she's not having my soup,' she added with a half-hearted chuckle.

Ruby picked up her spoon and smiled at Erin, sheepishly. 'Thank you, Mummy.'

Erin smiled back but said nothing. She remembered having an imaginary friend as a child, shortly after the death of her parents. Tom was his name. She recalled them playing together, brave knights and fair maidens if she remembered correctly. They used to get into all sorts of mischief. She supposed imaginary friends were completely natural, just a normal part of childhood. She looked across the table at Ruby and smiled. Ruby smiled back, wiping a drop of soup from her chin. She leaned over and pretended to wipe a spot of soup from her imaginary friend's face as well.

'There, that's better,' Ruby said and finished what remained of her dinner.

Erin stacked her empty bowl on top of Ruby's and took them over to the sink to wash. She could hear Ruby singing to herself as she gathered her paper and crayons from the dresser in the living room. Drawing was one of her favourite things to do, and Erin glanced over at the fridge door, already covered in colourful pictures, and wondered where she could find room to place this new masterpiece. She began to dry her hands on the blue and white striped towel hanging beside the sink, but froze when she heard a loud bang from the living room, and raced for the door when she heard Ruby scream at the top of her voice. She entered the living room to find Ruby crouched on the floor, her hand stuck in the dresser drawer.

'Ruby? Baby, are you alright?' Erin asked, rushing over and opening the drawer, releasing Ruby's hand. She took her daughter into her arms and smoothed her hair away from her face. She gently lifted Ruby's hand. A dark red bruise was already forming a line across the top. 'Ooh sweetie, this looks sore,' she said and gently kissed the top of her head.

'Eleanor...tol...told me...to sh...sh...shut my hand in the drawer,' Ruby whimpered, barely able to get her breath.

'What?' Erin pulled back a little to look at Ruby. 'Look, you're not in trouble, Ruby. You don't need to make up stories. But you must promise me that you will never, ever hurt yourself like that again.' Erin stared directly into Ruby's eyes.

'I'm not making up stories, Mummy,' Ruby sobbed, burying her face in Erin's shoulder.

Erin wrapped her arms around her daughter and gently rocked her back and forth. When Ruby's cries had reduced to the occasional sniffle and hiccup Erin checked her daughter's hand more closely. Reassured there were no broken bones she stood, still holding Ruby in her arms, and carried her over to the sofa and laid her down.

'Shall I get Mr Snuffles?' Erin asked. Ruby nodded, pitifully and popped her thumb into her mouth. Erin quickly retrieved Ruby's beloved, though slightly threadbare, white bunny from Ruby's bedroom. When she returned Ruby was fast asleep.

'Looks like an early night tonight, little one,' she whispered and carefully lifted Ruby and carried her upstairs to her small bedroom. Laying her down on her bed, Erin gently pulled off each of Ruby's shoes and placed them on the floor. She decided not to put her in her pyjamas tonight. One night really wouldn't hurt. She put Ruby to bed without waking her and tucked Mr Snuggles under the covers with her. Ruby rolled over, wrapping her arm tightly around him. Erin kissed her lightly on the cheek and crept out of the room, deciding herself that an early night would be the perfect opportunity to catch up on all that reading she had been meaning to do. Three pages later and Erin too was fast asleep.

* * *

Erin woke to the sound of giggling coming from Ruby's bedroom. A bright sword-shaped streak of light shone through a thin gap in the curtains, straight across her covers, as though cutting through her legs. Erin quickly pulled her legs towards her chest and listened. It sounded as though Ruby were having a full conversation, but her voice was too muffled to hear what she was saying. Erin swung her legs over the side of the bed and sat up, rubbing her eyes. She grabbed her dressing gown, hanging on the end of the bed, and put it on and made her way to Ruby's bedroom.

'Good Morning, sweetheart. How are you feeling this mor…' The words died in her mouth at the sight that greeted her when she opened the door. It appeared that every doll Ruby owned lay strewn across the bedroom floor or on the bed. Each doll's hair had been cut, or rather hacked off, leaving nothing but the odd wispy tuft on their once pretty heads. Some had holes the size of a pencil where the eyes once were and ominously grinning, dark slashes in place of their mouths.

'What have you done?' Erin croaked, barely able to speak.

Ruby sat in the centre of her bed and looked straight at her mother. 'Mummy it wasn't me. I promise I didn't do it. It was Eleanor.'

Erin walked over beside Ruby and picked up the pair of scissors lying on the bed. 'I have told you never to touch my scissors. They're very sharp and extremely dangerous.' Looking closer at Ruby, she asked. 'When did you put your nightgown on?'

'Last night. Eleanor said that it isn't ladylike to wear daytime clothes to bed. That I need to stop being a baby. So, I don't need Mr Snuffles anymore.' Ruby looked down at her hands, biting her bottom lip, trying her hardest not to cry.

Erin sat down on the bed beside her and placed her arm around her daughter's little shoulders. 'Hey, you can have Mr Snuffles for as long as you like.'

'Even when I am as old as you?' Ruby asked, with a cheeky giggle.

'Even when you are as old as me,' Erin laughed, kissing the top of Ruby's head. 'Where is Mr Snuffles?' she asked, looking all around the room.

'Eleanor threw him out the window. He is caught in the branches of the cherry tree.'

'Ruby!' Erin spoke more harshly than she meant to. 'That was silly.'

'But...' Ruby began as Erin drew the curtains and opened the window.

'I can reach that from here,' Erin said as she lifted herself up onto the window ledge. She shuffled out as far as she could whilst holding onto the window frame with her left hand. Stretching out with her right arm she reached for the white rabbit. She was close, only a centimetre or so away. She carefully shuffled a little farther and stretched her arm out as far as she could. Just as she felt the soft yet threadbare Mr Snuffles beneath her fingers, she heard a whisper in her ear.

'Won't you play with us?'

Erin spun around, her heart beating wildly in her chest. A small boy with blond hair stared back, a wicked grin revealing blackened teeth.

'I remember you,' Erin gasped, her eyes wide. 'You're Tom.'

'Wrong. I'm not Eleanor either,' it said as its face morphed into that of a pretty young girl, but with eyes of solid black. It uttered a laugh so inhuman it made Erin's skin crawl. It peeled her fingers one by one from the edge of the window. Erin screamed as she reached around desperately grasping for the window with her other hand. The tips of her fingers brushed the edge, but it was no use. She fell to the ground below, as if in slow motion.

It's not true what they say. Her life did not flash before her eyes. Just terror, confusion and intense love for her daughter. She lay for a moment looking up through the branches of the cherry tree blowing gently in the morning breeze, then closed her eyes and dreamt of brave knights and fair maidens.

JENNY

Phillip Tomasso

I didn't think I could kill myself sober.

I'd spent the last half hour strolling the aisles of the liquor store, just letting my eyes run over the endless rows of labels. I started out looking at gins and vodkas. I moved into an aisle with just tequilas and then moved, quickly, on to the next. A tequila intoxication was never pleasant.

An aisle over was filled with whiskey, scotch, and bourbons. Five shelves lined each side of the lane with ten to fifteen different brands on each shelf. I knew nothing about any of this. It was more like judging a book by its cover. I picked up a bottle for closer inspection based on the name of the booze and how much I liked the label design.

"Can I help you?" The guy I'd seen behind the counter when I entered the store now stood at the end of the aisle closest to the checkout. The store clerk kept one hand in his pocket as if the request for assistance were casual. It was the other hand, the one he didn't know what to do with, that made his intentions clearer.

I got it. I'd been in the store a while and was probably making the guy nervous as fuck. Truth, I needed help, regardless of whether he thought I might be stealing. "You know what? Yes, you can."

The tension, in his otherwise stiff stance, loosened. Some. He took the hand out of his pocket as he walked toward me. "Of course. What, exactly, are you looking for?"

I pulled a bottle of Longbranch Wild Turkey off the shelf. Showed him the label.

He nodded with complete approval. "That's a popular whiskey."

Music played from speakers set into the ceiling tiles. I knew the song. It played on both pop and country radio stations. I could sing along getting most of the words right, but for the life of me couldn't think of the artist or the song title. I hated that.

"McConaughey says it's a bourbon." My mind combed through memories for the name of the tune cascading down from above.

"Ah, who?"

"McConaughey. Matthew. The actor-guy."

"Ah, yeah. Well, it is. It's a bourbon-whiskey."

I shifted the bottle from one hand into the other so I could closely examine the label. "I'm not getting it."

"It's considered both a bourbon and a whiskey."

"What's the difference between bourbon, whiskey and a, what is the other thing? The other one?" I asked.

"Scotch," he said.

"Right. Is there a difference between bourbon, whiskey, and scotch?" I asked. "Rascal Flatts."

"What?"

"Nothing. The song," I said, pointing up at the ceiling.

"That's the artist."

"That's what I meant. Artist," I said. "Know the song?"

The clerk looked at me, his head tilted to one side. The movement reminded me of a dog. My parents had a German Shepherd that cocked its head to one side when someone asked her a question. "These Days?"

I clapped my free hand on my thigh, careful not to drop the bottle. "That's right. That's it. These Days. Good song."

"What had you asked me?"

"The name of the song?" I said, this time cocking my head to one side.

"No, about the bourbon."

"Oh," I said. "Yeah. Is there a difference between like whiskey, bourbon, and scotch?"

He looked more comfortable talking about booze. I hated thinking I made him apprehensive, unless he was always just a bit socially awkward. "Ah, yeah. That's right. Of course, there is. The biggest question of whether you are drinking a whiskey or a bourbon is a federal thing."

"Federal?"

"Yep. It comes down to grains and the overall proof of the alcohol. The difference between scotch and whiskey is geography. You know, where it's distilled. Also, some of the ingredients are different. And naturally, their spelling."

"Spelling?"

"Yeah. Like whiskey is w-h-i—"

"No, I get that. They're not spelled the same."

"Exactly. That makes them different."

"That's just obvious, though," I said.

"Well, I suppose. But did you know that?"

"That bourbon isn't spelled anything like scotch? Yeah. I knew that." I strained all of the muscles in my face as I desperately tried not to roll my eyes. I don't think I succeeded, though. "So basically the three are the same?"

"No." The store clerk shook his head. This time I think I caught him rolling his eyes. "Not at all."

The caramel colored booze made me feel thirsty. Unfortunately, drinking the swill made me drool before the liquid touched my lips. The smell alone made my mouth salivate, but not in a oh, this looks delicious kind of way. Back when I was twelve, I used to spend the night over at my friend Danny's house. We lived on the same street, a small housing tract in the town of Gates. Even though we went to different schools, we grew up as best friends. His parents were very social. They went out most weekends. Since Danny had older brothers and a sister, his parents didn't bother with babysitters, and his older siblings never bothered with us.

We'd get into mischief all the time. The thing we liked to do most was drink. Danny's father had a pretty healthy collection of alcohol that he never seemed to touch. Danny would always select this milkshake glass for our evenings. We would fill it with a horrid concoction of Southern Comfort – I have no idea if that is a whiskey, bourbon or scotch – beer and wine. Stir it up with a spoon, and then we would drink it out of a Crazy Straw.

Most of those nights we spent taking turns bent over the toilet throwing up. Imagine being twelve years old and promising God you'd never drink again between heaves? It was how I spent my weekends. The lesson was never learned.

"People tend to like this one, this brand?" I hoisted the McConaughey bottle in the air and then lowered it.

"They do."

Vivid memories of spitting up a mouthful of pooled saliva after chugging Southern Comfort from the bottle on the railroad tracks at the end of Charlene Drive with Danny convinced me to set the McConaughey back on the shelf. "You know what? Think I am going to pop in next door and just grab a twelve-pack of beer."

* * *

The Rochester Port Apartments, once the Holy Cross Elementary School, sat on the corner of Latta Road and Lighthouse Street, about fifty yards north of the Charlotte-Genesee Lighthouse. The four-story building was newly renovated and meant to attract low-income families, which was why and how I could afford to live here.

The place quickly became known as the Section 8 Tower. Landlords leased the units to pre-approved poor people, and the U.S. Department of Housing and Urban Development picked up the difference in paying rent.

I had a studio in the basement. Did that make it a five-story building? The place might have had a sub-basement, too. If it did, I didn't think anyone lived below me. I had no idea if basement and sub-basement levels counted when talking about stories. Entering the first-floor lobby from the back entrance with a twelve-pack of beer under my arm, I decided I didn't really care if this was a high-rise or not. In a year or two, my money was on the place becoming a complete shithole. I knew my car wasn't safe in the back parking lot whether I locked the doors or not, and I didn't feel safe in my apartment with windows in line with the ground. The postage-stamp-sized apartment, with a bed in my living room/kitchenette, was closer to a slightly oversized coffin than it was to a humble abode.

I didn't consider it home. It was just a place to live. Seeing as today was it for me, it didn't matter one way or the other.

Inside the apartment, I set the beer down on the counter. I tore into the cardboard box and extracted two bottles. Using my shirt as a buffer, I twisted off the cap of the first and flung it into the sink. It clattered around as I downed the alcohol in three big gulps. As I belched with content, I opened the second bottle and flicked that cap into the sink, as well.

Slowly, I spun around taking in my studio. I'd lived here six months and hadn't hung a single picture frame. Most of my stuff was still stuffed inside boxes in the caged storage area down the hall near the community washing and drying machines.

Craigslist ads led me to a slightly used sofa-bed, an artistically scratched-up dresser, and a flat screen television. My guitar sat on a guitar stand in the corner. It needed new strings, but I haven't had the desire to play it in months.

I took a seat at the kitchen counter on the tall stool, finished the second beer and started right in on the third.

The burping picked up between long sips. Soon enough I would have to pee. In a funny, albeit odd, way, I looked forward to urinating. It was most times one of those simple pleasures that brought about a calming relief. The best urination experiences were always followed up with shivers that started in the shoulders and wiggled through my arms and back.

Standing in front of the toilet, lid up, I gave it a go. While the actual act did indeed please me, there were no orgasmic-like shivers that I'd hoped for.

From beside the small refrigerator, I grabbed the three-step stool, and took it into the living room/bedroom. I used the remote and turned the television on. I streamed *Ancient Aliens* on Hulu before affixing the rope over the rafter. I made the noose myself. I used to think tying a Windsor knot was perplexing. Thank God for YouTube.

Standing on the top stair on the stool, I fitted my face inside the noose as a final check and rested my chin in the bow of the rope. It was the perfect size for my head. I climbed down from the stool and went back to the kitchen counter for another beer.

I went back to beside the noose, draped an arm through the hoop, and drank down my fourth beer. Giorgio listed cold hard facts about why we're not alone in the universe. I never thought we were. Seemed idiotic believing with all of the billions of suns and planets out there that life – intelligent life – existed only on Earth. It was like faith. Sometimes you don't have to see to believe. Sometimes you just know the truth, whether you could prove something or not. Better still, Tsoukalos agreed with me.

I completed a slow three-sixty. One box in a corner was all that mattered in my life. The rest could be tossed in a dumpster when I was gone.

I thought about a note and even started writing one a few times. I found it always came out sounding more authorly than sincere. When I'd read out loud the words I'd written it made me cringe. If anyone cared about me when I was gone, a goodbye letter wouldn't make a bit of difference.

I didn't expect many to care, anyway.

* * *

After I fitted my head through the oval opening of the noose, I made sure the knot rested against the bulbose spot on my spine on the back of my neck. The idea of pain frightened me. I wanted to kick away the step stool and drop fast. The neck needed to snap fast. I did not need to asphyxiate myself to death.

It doesn't mean I didn't try figuring out a better, faster way to do this.

I had heard too many horror stories about attempted suicides with a rifle. The brain gets chunked away with hunks of skull, but the person survives but finds themselves now a para- or quadriplegic. How fucked up would that be? It would just prove, once again, I was a failure at something else.

There was the ever-popular warm bath, razor blades, and bleeding out in the tub scenario. Sounded generally painless, minus the initial slashes, of course. Death came slowly. I worried I'd work up the nerve to cut through veins and arteries, but then second guess the decision and end up calling 911 for help.

I needed a plan with no turning back.

I didn't have a handgun. Despite ridiculous news reports, I didn't know how to get my hands on one illegally, either.

Poison seemed like a long, drawn-out process that might or might not work.

There was no way I could jump off the top of a building. I wouldn't even leap into a swimming pool in the middle of summer when it felt like a hundred degrees outside. I'd have to first dip my toe in the water, multiple times, before surrendering the idea of jumping and instead just climbing down the pool ladder one agonizing wrung at a time.

Hanging seemed like the last, and best, resort.

I held the noose under my chin with one hand. The other gave the length of rope a tug, ensuring everything was snug and ready to go.

Which it was.

And then I heard her crying . . .

* * *

It sounded like someone in the apartment next door was crying. I did not realize anyone lived in the apartment next door. When I swallowed, I was aware of my Adam's apple as it passed the grip of the rope.

The crying became louder. The woman was sobbing. It had absolutely nothing to do with me.

I stepped off the stool.

The rope tightened around my neck. The abrasive twine-like texture cut into my skin, but my neck didn't immediately snap as I'd hoped.

My feet kicked around, as I gasped for air.

I couldn't get anything into my lungs. My eyeballs were opened wide.

This was it. My moment. My end.

Yet, all I could hear, above the hammering of my heart inside my skull, was the cries from the woman next door. It shouldn't matter. Her crying was irrelevant. Talk about stealing the thunder.

My feet dangled. The rope held. My body twisted. It almost felt like I was flying, or falling.

The cries became even louder and more intense.

Realizing I could take two minutes and check on her, before finishing what I'd started, I snatched the pocket knife out of my pocket. It wasn't easy, but I managed to grab onto the rope above my head with my left hand to hoist myself up, and with my right, I sawed at the rope with my knife.

The noose was too tight around my throat. I thought I might black out before the teeth on the blade could sever the rope.

Just when I was certain I would black out, the rope gave and my body collapsed in a heap on the floor. I rolled onto my back and then to my side, coughing. My lungs fought for air. When I could finally suck in deep, long breaths, my head cleared. The room stopped spinning, and I could raise myself up onto an elbow without passing out.

I made a clicking noise with my tongue and the roof of my mouth. I had been that close. That close.

I retrieved another beer before I left my place and stepped out into the hallway.

Outside the apartment next to mine, I set my ear against the door. Whoever was on the other side was still crying. After a brief hesitation, my knuckles poised ready to rap on the door, I decided I would make this quick. See what's what and get out.

I knocked.

The crying stopped.

"Hello?" I said, my mouth by the wood door. I didn't want to yell.

The door opened a crack. The chain lock still engaged. I looked at a fragment of blue eyeball looking out at me. "Yes?" she said.

I stood back from the door – less imposing this way – and folded my arms. "I, ah, I live next door."

"I know who you are," she said. Aside from the sliver of eye, with a curly tangle of blond hair above her forehead, there was just the hint of full, red lips.

She knew who I was, and I thought the apartment next to me was vacant. Made sense. It lent credence to the fact I was not truly alert. My situational awareness was for shit. "Yeah, well I heard you – I heard someone crying."

The woman bit down on her lip. It seemed like she might want to tell me to get lost. Instead, she shut the door. I heard the chain slide free. The door opened.

The lights were off in the apartment. She stood just far enough back that the triangle of artificial light from the hallway didn't touch her. Draped in shadow, she stood with her arms at her sides. She wore a white tank top and blue jeans. I tried not noticing she did not have on a bra. It wasn't easy averting my gaze. Stammering when uncomfortable came naturally to me. "I… I just… I wanted to make sure everything was okay."

"That was nice of you. I'm sorry I bothered you," she said. "I hope I didn't interrupt something important."

Reflexively, my hand went to the back of my neck. "No, nothing that couldn't wait a few more minutes."

She smiled.

A silence filled the space between us.

I pointed toward my door, as she waved a hand. We said at the same time:

Me: "I suppose I should be going—"

Her: "Would you like to come in—"

And then we both answered each other simultaneously.

Her: "Of, course, I understand."

Me: "Sure, I guess so."

We both laughed.

She pulled open her door. "Come in?"

I walked in. "Thank you."

* * *

We sat on her sofa. She got two glasses from the cupboard. I poured my beer out in equal doses.

"Always travel with your own beer?"

"Never know when you are going to get thirsty." I raised my glass. We clinked them together and then took a sip and set them back down on coasters.

"Is it too dark in here?"

It was very dark. The two small basement windows let in what little light was left from the day. Everything coated in a gloom, aside from the woman seated beside me. Her eyes looked brilliant and alive. "It's fine. Why were—"

"What were you doing?"

We laughed. We'd done it again. Talked at the same time.

"Ah," I waved a dismissive hand.

"What would you say if I told you I knew what you were doing."

I tried smiling. This wasn't why I was here.

She touched my hand. I couldn't look away from her eyes. "Want me to tell you a story?" I asked.

"I would like that."

I liked how she held my hand, the way her skin felt on mine. More than that, I liked the way she was staring at me. It was as if she were genuinely interested. For some odd reason, I wanted to open up and share with her.

"I moved here about a year ago. Next door to you. I had a house."

"What happened to your house?"

"Oh, it's still there. My wife and my kids live in it. See, she was seeing someone else, but I didn't know this until it was too late."

"Too late?"

"Two years ago she stopped wearing her wedding ring. She also stopped telling me she loved me, even when I told her first," I said. "Should have told me there was something wrong. I mean seriously wrong."

"You didn't know?"

"I worked a couple of jobs. Put in terrible hours. I was trying to take care of my family." I let my head tip to one side, thinking. "I probably wasn't the most responsive husband. Okay, I know I wasn't. But we had debt. Too much debt. I was doing everything I could to take care of my family."

"She must have known this."

I snickered. "You would think. She didn't. She was already talking with another guy."

172

"She was?"

"It got to a point where I begged her to go to marriage counseling, to talk with the church pastor—"

"And what did she say?"

"She said no."

"So what did you say?"

"That I wanted a divorce."

"Do your kids know this, how it happened?"

"I never told them all of that. They don't need to know all of those details."

"No. I suppose they don't."

"I moved out."

"You moved next door."

I nodded. I drained my glass.

"You miss your kids?"

"I miss my life."

"Your wife?"

"I don't miss her," I said. I eyed her glass. I was so thirsty.

There was a loud knocking on the door. Not her door.

I got to my feet.

She grabbed my arm. Her touch sent an electrical current through my body that slammed into my heart in a way I had not felt in some time. "Stay here," she said.

I could not take my eyes off her. "Someone's at my door."

I opened her door. There was no one in the hall. My apartment door was open. Inside my apartment was a police officer and the super.

A body dangled from a rope from the rafters.

The officer bent down and picked up a pocket knife from the floor.

I turned around.

She was waiting for me. "Come back with me."

I ran into my apartment and passed through the officer. My face was blue, and my eyes were popping out of the sockets. "Is that me? Am I dead?"

She frowned.

"That's me. I'm dead."

She touched my shoulder. "Come back with me."

* * *

We walked into her apartment.

She led me, holding my hand, pulling me along.

We stopped once inside, once the door behind us closed.

The bathroom door was open. The only light in the apartment came from that room. Like a moth, I was drawn toward the room.

From behind, she grabbed my arm. "Don't go in there."

My steps were slow. Shuffles. "Who are you?"

"My name is Jenny," she said. She stayed behind me. She stood statue-still.

I reached the bathroom and looked inside.

Jenny was naked in a tub filled with blood and water. One arm hung out over the tiled floor. The gashes on her wrist went from the palm of her hand up toward her elbow.

I dropped onto my knees.

She put her hands on my shoulders. I looked up. She was standing over me.

"You heard me crying. I started when I realized what you were about to do in your apartment," Jenny said.

"You knew?"

"I sensed it," she said. "I have been sensing your pain for months now."

"I heard you crying. I stopped. I cut myself down."

"You tried."

I lowered my head. I saw blood like grout joining the small square floor tiles. "I tried."

The silence between us…

"Now what?"

She knelt down beside me. "Now this."

I looked at her blue eyes. They seemed less brilliant, less alive. "What's this?"

She nodded. "This is our forever," she said. She smiled.

"Why are you smiling, Jenny?"

"Don't be angry with me, please. I know it's selfish of me," she said as she placed her hand on mine. "But I'm no longer alone."

I sighed and gave her hand a gentle squeeze. There was no way I was good with any of this, yet. I'd need time. "You're going to have to help me along. Show me the…"

Jenny smiled. Her blue eyes lit up. She laughed. "Show you the ropes?"

I laughed as we got up. I started closing the bathroom door. "Jenny?" I said. "What happened in here?"

AMY

Donna L. Greenwood

'Come on, Dawn, for God's sake, don't be such a wuss. It'll be a laugh.' Jerry let go of my hand and climbed the rickety gates of the North Pier. He dropped to the ground on the other side like a circus acrobat and did a little bow for me. 'Come on. It's easy.'

Jerry McCullen – long dark hair, a swagger on his hips and a curl on his lips – God, he was as sweet and cool as ice cream and he was out on a Friday night with *me*. I looked up at the chained gates. The pier looked different in winter. It looked nasty. Haunted. I hated the place. Old wives said that only fools went to the pier at night. After three tragic deaths, rumours had spread like plague and there was a glut of warnings to teenagers about staying away from the place. But, I was on a date with Jerry McCullen and I didn't want to blow it. I put the strap of my bag across my body to free my hands and started climbing the gates. Jerry was right; it was easy. I dropped from the top of the gates and landed on my feet next to him. He smiled and kissed me softly on my lips.

'Impressive – for a girl.' And then he ran off, laughing.

'Don't...' I said, and then gave up. He'd already disappeared into the shadows of the amusement arcade. I stood for a while, taking in the surroundings. I could hear the soft susurration of the waves splashing against the legs of the pier and, further away, the faint tinkles of laughter and late night drunk-talk on the streets of Blackpool. I felt alienated from the chattering, northern humanity parading itself outside the gates of the pier. Here, I was alone with the dark and the breath of the wind. The moon was a too-bright gash in the inky black night. It cast skeletal shadows on the wooden slatted floor of the pier. I swallowed a small surge of unease and walked towards the closed arcade. I knew that Jerry would be hiding behind a corner, waiting to jump out and scare me, so I readied myself for him.

The North Pier was unlike its two sister piers in that there was nothing much to it. There was an amusement arcade at the start of the pier and then a long stretch of wooden boards before you reached a few pretty Victorian kiosks. There was also a bar at the end of the pier and, in summer, there were a few rides, but, compared to its whorish sisters, the Central and South Piers, the North Pier was like a faded old lady, restrained and low key. *And evil*, whispered a voice at the back of my mind. I immediately dismissed the voice by shouting out 'Jerry!' at the top of my lungs. Noise was the best antidote to those kinds of thoughts. Of course, he didn't reply. He was probably sniggering behind a kiosk somewhere, finding himself hilarious. I walked past the arcade, ready for him to jump out at me. Nothing happened. No Jerry. Just the *shush shush* of the waves and the flickering chiaroscuro of water shadows climbing the boards on the pier. I let out my breath a little. The arcade looked abandoned, even though it had only been closed for a few weeks. The windows had been boarded up and the happy yellow bubble writing that proclaimed NORTH PIER ARCADE over the top of the doors looked sick and treacly in the night light. The pier had been drained of all colour; even the wooden boards looked different. They looked like coffins. *Don't trust those boards*, a voice whispered. I shook my head. Stop it. Don't think about that. That happened years ago. The boards are safe. You're not going to…

Dawnie…

I whirled around. The voice was at my ear. An intimate whisper. And it wasn't Jerry's voice; it was softer. *Younger.*

'Hello?' I said. There was nothing behind me, just the Victorian benches lining the side of the pier and, in the distance, the illuminated Blackpool Tower.

'Dawn!' This time it *was* Jerry. He seemed so far away. 'Dawn, come on!'

'Jerry, wait for me!' I yelled and started to run, but when I felt the boards creak beneath me, I stopped. The boards on the pier were old; everyone knew that. There'd been accidents. I shut my eyes, determined that the memory would not surface.

Dawnie…

Dawnie…

My eyes sprung open. The wind had suddenly picked up. The waves were no longer gently pushing themselves against the legs of the pier; they were smashing and grabbing upwards. I could see sprays of water jetting through the gaps in the floor. Out of the corner of my eye, I caught a movement.

'Jerry?'

There was no answer. I looked at the kiosk and then sucked in a breath when I saw movement once again. A flash of red ran behind one of the kiosks. I knew it wasn't Jerry. A whimper escaped from my mouth. In the darkness, I could see a shape behind the warped glass of the kiosk. It was a face, a small, white face. *The face of a child.* There was a flash of red beneath the face.

She's wearing her red dress.

It's Amy.

'Jerry, for God's sake, where are you?' I screamed above the now roaring wind. I looked back at the arcade. I could go back. I could just go home, but then, I was out with Jerry freeking McCullen. I gave myself a little shake and moved onwards towards the bar at the end of the pier. Jerry must be in there, probably trying to break in and find some left-over alcohol.

It wasn't my fault.

Shit. Why did my mind keep going back to *that?* It happened over twelve years ago.

I was only little. It wasn't my fault.

For God's sake, put it away, Dawn; it's in the past. I hugged my black pleather jacket nearer to me. It was useless for keeping out the cold north wind. Just beneath the wind, I heard a commotion and the sound of glass smashing. It was coming from the bar. Jerry. I moved quickly in that direction, not looking at the kiosks lining the pier like crouching, crystal phantoms.

The moon had disappeared behind thickening clouds by the time I'd reached the shuttered bar at the end of the pier. The night was as black as pitch and there was no sign of Jerry. I sat on one of the wooden benches at the side of the pier and looked into my bag for Jerry's cigarettes. I'd been pleased when he'd asked me to look after his stuff – a lighter, some fags and his phone. It'd made me feel like a proper girlfriend, although it now meant I had no way of contacting him. I found his cheap Lambert and Butler's and pinched one. I lit it with his black zippo lighter. Jerry was very cool. I smiled and took a drag on the cigarette. Jerry had to be somewhere. This was all part of some elaborate joke.

Dawnie…

I threw my fag down and looked up.

Dawnie

The voice was coming from the other side of the bar. There was someone hiding behind the small shack-like pier bar.

Dawnie

I screwed up my eyes to try and see better in the dark. Was there a shape coming out from behind the wall?

'Jerry?'

In the dark shadows, again I saw a smear of red. *She's wearing her red dress.* I pressed my back into the bench. It, *she,* was emerging from behind the wall. I saw one thin arm curl around the wooden shack, and then another appeared. I didn't want to see her face. I didn't want to see Amy's face. Instead, I looked at her ragged red dress as she emerged from the darkness. She was wearing that red dress twelve years ago. Twelve years ago on her birthday.

* * *

It was my big sister's birthday, and we were celebrating with a day out at the pier.

AMY

'Come on, Dawnie!' Amy was saying, pulling me along the pier. My parents were miles behind. They'd had a glass of wine in the bar and they were laughing into one another's eyes, and I felt so happy because they were happy. I let myself be pulled along by Amy's hands. Amy's nails were digging into my skin. She always liked to inflict a little pain on me when our parents were distracted. I let it go; I didn't want to ruin Mum and Dad's happiness. I let Amy scratch up my arms. I'd tell on her later.

'Come on, Dawnie. Let's go right to the end of the pier. Let's go whale watching!' I was only five but even I knew that there weren't any whales in Blackpool, but I played along with her. Amy was not only three years older than me, she was really big for her age. It was impossible for me to pull my hand away from my sister. We reached the end of the pier and Amy let go of my hand. We both stared out at the sea for a moment and then Amy snatched my candy floss from my hands and shouted, 'Mine now!' into my face. Then she pushed me hard in my belly and I crashed against the barrier.

'Amy! That hurt.'

'You big baby. It was only a little push.'

Amy was standing about a foot away from me. She was shovelling my candy floss into her mouth, looking pleased with herself, when there was a creaking sound beneath us. I felt the ground begin to move and held onto the barrier. Amy had nothing to hold onto. The boards beneath her popped and cracked and big gaping holes began to appear around her. She dropped my candy floss and began to run towards me, her arms outstretched. Suddenly, there was loud, splintering sound and the board that Amy was standing on disappeared. Amy's eyes bore into mine as she slipped

181

through the gap. Her arm flung out before her and she managed to grab my ankle just as her body fell through the hole. Her long nails ripped into my skin. She looked up at me, her mouth and eyes wide open.

'Dawnie, grab my hand!' she was screaming, her other hand flailing around in the air. More boards were falling into the sea around me and Amy's fingers were hurting. Without thinking, I used my other foot to kick away Amy's hand from my ankle. She held on tight, so I kicked it again. And again. Until she eventually let go. I screamed as my big sister fell through the hole and into the sea. The last expression I saw on Amy's face wasn't terror. It was absolute, bloody fury.

* * *

I closed my eyes and tried to dislodge the memory. I was only a little girl and I was afraid of Amy; she was so big, she would have dragged me down with her. *I'm so sorry, Amy,* I mouthed to the apparition crawling towards me in the dark. The red dress disintegrated before me. Tiny shreds of my sister blew away in the wind. I was alone once more. I stood and walked towards the bar. I could hear another noise. It sounded like Jerry.

'Help, Dawn. Help me.'

He sounded weak and frightened. Not like Jerry at all. Panic drilled through my bones.

'I'm here, Jerry. I'm here. Where are you?'

And then, I swear to God, I heard Jerry McCullen crying. That made me move fast. I ran towards the sound of his cries. They were coming from behind the bar, towards the end of the pier where... *where you murdered your sister.*

182

Around the corner, in the darkness, I could see nothing at first and then, oh my God, Jerry... I ran towards him and then stopped. I didn't want to disturb the boards any more than they already were; I tip-toed a little closer. Jerry was in front of me. Or at least half of him was. The other half of him was hanging through a hole in the pier's wooden boards. He'd managed to stop the rest of his body falling through the boards by hooking out both of his elbows. He was now valiantly trying to haul himself back up again but, every time he did, the boards groaned a little more, threatening to give way. I slowly pulled out my phone from my bag.

'Don't panic. Try not to move. I'll call an ambulance or the fire brigade or something...'

'No, just get your ass over here and pull me up. Come on, for Christ's sake.' He was still crying, but there was anger in his voice. I inched forwards a little, but I could feel the boards begin to move beneath me. Tears were streaming down my face. I couldn't believe this was happening again.

Dawnie...

The voice, Amy's voice, was directly underneath me. I looked down. Beneath the boards, I saw her eyes staring up at me. They were red and angry. Long, grey fingers curled up through the boards between my feet. She grabbed hold of my ankle, her jagged, uncut fingernails digging into the flesh there. I screamed and kicked her away. I stamped my feet onto the ground. The wooden slats began to creak more loudly.

Dawnie...

Her voice was further away. She was near Jerry.

'Dawn, for God's sake, just come over here and help

me,' Jerry was screaming. His mouth and eyes were wide with panic. From beneath him, two grey arms curled up through the hole. They snaked around his arms and elbows.

'Amy!' I yelled.

The disembodied arms grabbed Jerry around his neck and pulled. I watched as Jerry McCullen fell through the hole in the pier and into the sea below. He didn't even have time to scream. I ran towards the gap and flung myself down on my knees. I looked through smashed up floorboards. Amy was sat on the scaffolding beneath the pier. Her body was emaciated and grey. I couldn't see her face because her head was bent over the broken body of my boyfriend. She was stroking his face with her dirty fingers. He was still alive. He looked up at me, his eyes full of pain and confusion. Amy's head jolted back and she stared up at me. Her eyes were gone. Her toothless maw opened wide and two words came shrieking out and echoed around the crumbling pier.

Mine now!

She hooked her arms around his neck and the two of them plummeted into the crashing waves below.

I sat on the boards for a while. I waited for the wind to die down and the waves to calm, and then I picked up Jerry's phone and cigarettes and lighter and threw them into the sea. I took a deep breath and made my way to the front of the pier where I would use my key to open the gate. She was my sister; anyone would do the same. And it stopped the dreams, those bloody awful nightmares where Amy finally hooks her claws into my ankles and pulls me down with her. I no longer questioned it. On nights like this, it was easy. There were plenty of stray boys in Blackpool and it didn't take much for a pretty girl to persuade them to go to the North Pier with her, despite what the old wives say.

THE SCRAMBLER

Jill Hand

There's a first time for everything and at 10:38 P.M. on April 23, 2019, it was Cindi Trauben's first time at drunk dialing. Cindi had consumed three glasses of wine, two more than her usual single after-dinner glass to reward herself for a day spent cleaning out the hoarder's nest that was her mother-in-law's house

The two extra glasses of Chablis were partly the fault of a text from her brother-in-law and partly because Cindi had been reunited with the Scrambler.

She rinsed her dinner plate of traces of pasta carbonara and got up unsteadily to put it in the dishwasher. There was a note Scotch-taped to the front in her mother-in-law's shaky handwriting. It said *Do not run until full. Water bill is TOO HIGH!* The last two words were not only capitalized but underlined for emphasis.

Cindi considered the red telephone on the kitchen counter. "I wonder if you still work?" she asked it.

The Scrambler was what they always called the red phone. Cindi wasn't sure why, although it may have been so dubbed by her Uncle Ronnie, who'd been in the Air Force. It was one of those special words all families seem to have, a private way of referring to an object or event.

"Who was that on the Scrambler just now?" her grandmother would say, entering the dining room and seeing someone hanging up the receiver. Or Cindi's father, fishing off the dock, would tilt his head beneath his wide-brimmed sun hat in the direction of the cottage and ask, "Is that the Scrambler ringing?"

Cindi had last seen the Scrambler in 1979, that final summer at her grandparents' cottage on Messalonskee Lake. Now it was back.

Cindi knew it was the same phone despite the passage of forty years. She recognized it immediately from the scorch mark on one side. The black bubbly mark resembled the silhouette of a pelican. It had been caused by her Cousin Matt fooling around with a cigarette lighter, way back when Nixon was president.

Where it had been for the past forty years was unknown. Cindi encountered it in an antique shop in Waldoboro, Maine. The shop had a sign in front with *Weird Stuff, Cool Junk* written on it in funky pink and green nineteen-sixties-style lettering.

Cindi pulled up and parked her mother-in-law's black GMC Yukon. She'd driven the nineteen miles from her mother-in-law's house in Camden with the windows down, a bath towel protecting her jeans-clad bottom from contact with the driver's seat. That was due to the fact that the seat reeked of stale urine, despite having been sprayed repeatedly with Lysol. Cindi's mother-in-law had developed incontinence along with dementia. Numerous dents in the bumpers and sides of the big SUV bore witness to the fact that Evelyn Trauben had been in no shape to drive. Her children eventually managed to get the keys away from her while she clawed at them, shrieking like a banshee.

Now Evelyn was in a memory care unit at an assisted living facility in Oakland, where her exhausted children had lured her by telling her it was a resort where she'd won a free vacation. Now they were faced with the task of cleaning out Evelyn's house to prepare it for sale.

Or rather Cindi was faced with the task.

Evelyn had gone from antique collecting to full-on hoarding and the house and garage were crammed full of stuff. Everything had to be examined to make sure it didn't contain anything important, like the phone book from 2002 with forty-six ten-dollar bills tucked between its pages, or the box of instant oatmeal in one of the kitchen cabinets. Inside Cindi discovered a drawstring bag containing Evelyn's diamond engagement ring and a 14-karat gold bracelet.

A person in the right frame of mind might consider it an exciting adventure, a type of treasure hunt, but Cindi had passed that optimistic state a week ago. She'd been clearing out the refrigerator and had found a baby food jar filled with toenail clippings in the compartment on the door intended for holding sticks of butter.

The stark horror of that moment made her drop all pretense that she was having fun. Holding the jar filled with the curling half-moons of Evelyn's yellow toenails at arm's length, Cindi was forced to acknowledge that going through a hoarder's cache is a revolting business filled with nasty surprises.

On top of everything else, rats had taken up residence in the basement, where they'd made nests in the bundles of old newspapers and *National Geographics* that Evelyn had stubbornly refused to throw out. The exterminator was there that morning, and Cindi seized the opportunity to escape. She'd go for a drive in the Urine Mobile, since her own car was back home in New Jersey, and see if she could interest any of the antiques shops in Waldoboro in buying some of Evelyn's things.

A young woman in denim overalls, her hair dyed emerald green, was washing the front window of Weird Stuff, Cool Junk. She used a squeegee to whisk away the excess moisture as wind chimes suspended from the porch roof tinkled in the fresh, salt-scented air.

Cindi took a grateful breath, glad to be out of Evelyn's dusty, mothball-reeking house. The young woman nodded to her and greeted her with a "mawnin'." Cindi replied with a "mawnin'" of her own.

Whenever she spent more than a few days in Maine, Cindi's nasal New Jersey accent morphed into something leisurely and drawn-out, the Rs dropped altogether or softened until they sounded more like *ahs*. Her husband, Josh, teased her about it. She tried to stop herself from doing it, but was never completely successful.

That was because Cindi was a natural mimic. Her voice took on the characteristics of those around her. She could imitate Evelyn perfectly, something she took guilty pleasure in doing.

"Wheah's mah jahr of toenail clippins?" she said in Evelyn's voice as she went through dust-furred boxes in the attic filled with cancelled checks and Christmas cards from people who'd been dead for twenty years. Alone in the empty house she proclaimed, "Ahm goin' for a rahd in mah cawr. Ahm gonna pee in it!"

It was mean to mock an old lady with dementia, but Cindi didn't do it to be cruel; she was simply fed up. There was a lot of work to be done before the house was in a state where it could be sold. Nobody else was available to help her. Her brother-in-law Charles refused, saying he was too busy with his Brooklyn optometry practice. Charles' wife Barbara was also too busy, or so she claimed. She was Charles's office manager, and she often bragged to strangers about "my husband, the doctor." Cindi thought it would serve them both right if someone had a medical emergency in front of them and Charles had to confess that he wasn't a real doctor, just someone who fitted people for eyeglasses.

That left Josh, who was an accountant and was swamped at work with the tax deadline looming. Cindi worked from home as a freelance writer. That meant she was the one who got tapped to do the grunt work at Evelyn's.

"Do you mind if I look around?" Cindi asked the woman with green hair.

"Go on in," she replied, shaking off the squeegee before plunging it into the plastic bucket at her feet.

Cindi went in.

Looking around, Cindi saw the usual items found in antiques shops: the good (a breakfront filled with pieces of white opalescent hobnail cranberry glass) the bad (another breakfront filled with Precious Moments figurines) and the ugly (a selection of sixties and seventies kitsch.)

The woman with the green hair came in carrying the

squeegee and bucket. She set them down behind the counter. "It's wommin' up," she said. Cindi agreed that it was warming up.

"I'm clearing out my mother-in-law's house, over in Camden. She collected antiques. Would you be interested in some carnival glass, or Depression glass, things like that?" Cindi asked.

"Maybe. I'd have to see it," the woman said.

"There's a nice tiger maple roll-top desk, and eight place settings of Royal Crown Derby, and some Spode teacups and saucers. I'm having a yard sale, if you're interested," Cindi said.

"How about I look at what you've got before the yard sale? I can bring my partner. She knows about glassware," the woman said.

Cindi took the woman's business card and gave her the address and her phone number, pleased to have found a potential buyer. She was about to leave when she saw the Scrambler.

It used to be kept in the dining room of her grandparents' summer cottage, on what her grandmother called the occasional table. The table was made out of light-colored wood, most likely pine, by Cindi's grandfather. He had a workshop behind the boathouse where he liked to putter around and do woodworking.

Memories came flooding back: the clean, tangy scent of freshly cut lumber in her grandfather's workshop, and the sweet smell of his cherry pipe tobacco. She remembered the metallic smell of the lake and the gooshy feel of the sandy bottom between her toes. She remembered the rhythmic slap-slap of water hitting the pontoons beneath the floating dock.

Messalonskee Lake, she thought, and felt a shiver run up her backbone. Her grandparents had spent summers there since before World War II. They sold the cottage after that bad summer of 1979. Cindi had never been back.

She picked up the Scrambler from where it sat atop a display case, keeping one hand on the handset with its curly cord to prevent it from falling. The red plastic was still bright, the color of a ripe tomato. It was heavier than she remembered. Phones back then had been weighty. She'd forgotten how heavy they were, having grown used to her iPhone.

"That's forty dollars, but I could let you have it for thirty-six," the woman with the green hair told her.

"Thirty," Cindi said. She hadn't realized she wanted it until the word was out of her mouth.

The woman grinned. Dickering was a time-honored New England tradition, one its practitioners relished engaging in. "Thirty-five," she said.

After a little more back and forth, Cindi acquired the Scrambler for thirty-three dollars.

So, that night Cindi had three glasses of wine. Her indulgence in two extra glasses was also in part occasioned by the text from Charles. Her brother-in-law was hard to take at the best of times, officious and full of himself. He'd gotten worse since his mother went into assisted living. The text said: NEED YOU TO CONTACT THE BOSTON ATHENAEM. SEE IF THEY WANT MOM'S TENNYSON BOOKS. IT COULD MAKE A NICE TAX WRITE-OFF.

"Are you fucking kidding me?" Cindi said, staring at the screen in disgust.

Before her retirement Evelyn had taught English at

Colby College in Waterville. Her doctoral dissertation had been on Alfred Tennyson, author of "The Charge of the Light Brigade." Cindi supposed he was a big deal back in the day, but Evelyn's books were nothing special, not first editions, not signed by the great man himself or by any of his literary pals. The local library hadn't even wanted them. They were just old books, nothing to interest a prestigious place like the Athenaeum. She'd feel foolish approaching them, but she knew Charles; once he got an idea he never gave up.

"Why not?" she said. "While I'm at it why don't I call the Smithsonian and see if they want Evelyn's drawerful of plastic forks and spoons from McDonald's, and her vast, priceless collection of little packets of mustard and ketchup? I bet they'd jump at the chance to acquire those. What do you say to that, Chuck-o, old buddy?"

Charles, of course, didn't say anything to that because he was home in Brooklyn and couldn't hear her. Cindi shook her head. Then she noticed the Scrambler sitting on the kitchen counter. "I wonder if you still work?" she asked it.

The Scrambler sat there mutely.

"Let's see if you work," Cindi said.

Evelyn had a landline, a cell phone being too complicated for her. Cindi unplugged the flat grey cord connecting it to the phone jack in the wall above the kitchen counter. Then she plugged it into the back of the Scrambler. Lifting the handset she heard the steady hum of a dial tone.

"Eureka! We have liftoff!" she cried.

The question was who to call? She could call Josh, or one of her friends, but what she did instead, because it was the Scrambler and because she was a little drunk, was to dial the telephone number at her grandparents' cabin on the lake, just to see what would happen. Many surprising things have resulted down through the ages from people trying something just to see what would happen. In this case, what happened was the last thing Cindi expected.

Her sister Paula answered.

It was impossible. Paula was dead. She'd been dead since the summer of 1979, when she'd drowned at the age of nine. Yet it was her voice; Cindi recognized it immediately.

"H'lo? Campbell residence," the polite little voice said. Campbell was Cindi's maiden name. Her heart pounding, she said, "Paula? Is that you?"

"Yes. Who's this?"

Cindi gripped the handset, stunned. A glance in the mirror over the sink showed her that her face had turned ashen. Black spots bloomed before her eyes. *Don't faint,* she told herself. *It's just Paula. My God, how can it be Paula?*

"Who's this?" Paula repeated. "Is it Mrs. Macalusko? Is something wrong with Twinkles?"

Lucille Macalusko had been their next-door neighbor back home in Long Branch. She'd taken care of their cat, Twinkles, when they were in Maine.

Feeling numb, Cindi cleared her throat. Imitating her former neighbor's hoarse voice, the result of a two-pack-a-day Parliament habit, she said, "No, hon. Twinkles is fine. He's playing with his catnip mouse."

"You sound funny," Paula said.

"That's because I got one of them summer colds," Cindi told her.

A crackling sound of static came over the line. Fearing she'd lose the connection she said, "Quick, Paula, what day is it? What's today's date?"

"Saturday, August fourth. Why?"

"Nineteen seventy-nine?" Cindi asked. Her mouth felt dry as the Mohave Desert.

"Yeah. Is this a joke?" Paula laughed.

That was the day Paula drowned. She'd taken the canoe out without telling anyone. She hadn't been wearing a life vest and the canoe overturned. The rest of the family didn't realize what she'd done until it was too late.

Her voice shaking, Cindi spoke into the phone. "Listen, Paula. Don't take the canoe out by yourself today. Don't, please. Something very bad will happen if you do. I had a vision that you drowned. Please, promise me."

Amid the crackling static Cindi heard her sister say, "Okay."

The crackling turned into the steady hum of a dial tone. The call was over. Cindi's hand shook so that it took her two tries to get the handset in its cradle. Should she call back? Ask to speak with her grandmother, who'd died in 1985, or her grandfather, who'd died a year later, or one of her parents, both dead of cancer since the 1990s? Should she ask to speak to her younger self? What if she answered? What should she say?

The realization that she'd talked to her dead sister was staggering. A burning, sour lump rose in her throat as the pasta carbonara threatened to come back up. Cindi sprinted to the bathroom, where she leaned over the toilet and vomited.

After she finished throwing up she ran cold water in the sink and splashed her sweating face. Then she made a nest of blankets on the living room couch. Turning on the TV she watched old movies, one after another, trying not to think. Eventually she fell asleep.

The next morning Cindi's back was stiff from sleeping on the couch. Her head throbbed and she swallowed two aspirin with a glass of orange juice. She didn't want to look at the Scrambler, but she couldn't help it. *I talked to Paula last night,* she thought, eyeing the red telephone as if it were a coiled rattlesnake. *Or did I? I could have imagined it. It might have been a really intense dream.*

Who was she kidding? She knew it was no dream. Somehow, the Scrambler had connected her to her dead sister.

"You're a hoodoo," she told it, shivering.

Then she had a thought. If she'd convinced Paula not to take the canoe out on that long-ago afternoon, might she now be alive? She dug through her purse, searching for her smart phone.

She googled Paula Joan Campbell. Nothing came up. She tried Facebook, thinking her sister might have an account, but nothing came up there either. Maybe she'd gotten married and changed her name. Hardly daring to hope, she called Josh.

"Hey honey, how's it going?" he said. She could hear mingled voices in the background. Tax time was his busiest time of year. She tried to think how best to phrase the question she needed to ask.

"It's going, slowly but surely. I may have found somebody interested in buying your mom's glassware.

You know, I was thinking about Paula last night," she said.

"Uh-huh," he said. He sounded distracted, as if his mind was on someone's deduction that might or might not pass muster under the new tax laws. She plunged on. Choosing her words carefully, Cindi asked, "What did I tell you about her?"

"About your sister? Just that she died," he said, dashing her hope that Paula had survived.

"You mean she drowned," she said.

"No," he said, sounding surprised. "She had one of those diseases they have a cure for now, usually. I don't remember what it was. You said she was sick for a long time and then she died when you were in college."

She died when you were in college. The words shocked her. Paula had been nine when she drowned. Cindi was four years older. Cindi had been an August baby. She started college a month after she turned eighteen. That meant Paula lived at least another five years after that day at the lake.

The thought left her stunned. Five years! She'd had five more years with her only sibling, but she couldn't remember them. All her memories of Paula ended that terrible afternoon at the lake.

"Just reminiscing. Being back in Maine made me think of her. I'd better let you get back to the salt mines. Miss you," she said.

"Miss you, too," Josh said, and hung up.

Gripped with the need to find out what happened, Cindi went online and found her grandfather's obituary. After mentioning his six patents, his status as a thirty-third-degree Mason and his life membership in the

American Woodworker Hobbyists Association it got around to attributing his death in the fall of 1986 to "a long illness."

His wife and his granddaughter Paula had predeceased him in 1985. He was survived by two sons, a daughter, and six grandchildren.

There it was, spelled out in black and white. Six years. Paula had lived another six years after that day at the lake. There was one person she could rely on to fill in the blanks. Cindi took a deep breath and called her cousin Matt, the one responsible for the burn mark on the side of the Scrambler.

After the initial exchange of How've you been? How's the family? she got down to it.

"I was thinking about Paula," she said.

"Yeah. Awful thing," he said.

She asked, "Do you remember when she got sick?"

"Sure. I'll never forget it. Your mom called my mom and said she was taking her to the doctor. She said Paula had a fever and was complaining about her neck hurting. My mom, being a nurse, she went, 'Make sure they check her for meningitis. It's probably not, but you can never be too careful.' But that's what it was, poor kid. Later on, I remember my mom saying they had to amputate her arms and legs and how scared I was, thinking I'd get it too. Every time my neck felt stiff, I was convinced I had meningitis. To think she went through all that and died anyway. Horrible. Cindi, you still there?"

"I'm here," she croaked.

"Awful thing," he repeated. She could picture him shaking his head, his hair no longer thick and shoulder-length and blond – heavy metal hair – but short and gray and thinning on top. She and Matt were getting older. Someday they'd be gone too, but not yet. Now she had one more call to make. She hoped it wasn't too late.

"Say hi to Stephanie and the kids for me," she told him before hanging up.

She looked at the Scrambler. *She was sick for a long time. They had to amputate her arms and legs.*

"No," she whispered. "Hell no. That's not how it's gonna be."

It appeared there were two endings for her little sister, one by drowning and one by an agonizing, drawn-out illness. Drowning was bad, but at least it was quick, or so she hoped. Paula had been a pest at times, a tagalong and an occasional tattletale, but Cindi had loved her dearly.

She blew her nose. Then she picked up the handset and dialed.

The crackling was louder this time. She held her breath, willing the call to go through. After what felt like an eternity, it did.

"H'lo? Campbell residence," Paula said.

Cindi swallowed.

"Hi Paula," she said.

"Who's this? Is it Mrs. Macalusko? Is something wrong with Twinkles?"

It was like a reset of the last call.

"That's right, it's Mrs. Macalusko, hon," Cindi told her in Lucille Macalusko's raspy voice, trying not to start bawling again. "Twinkles is okay. I just called to see how you're all doing."

"We're fine. How are you?"

The crackling static was getting louder. Cindi had the feeling there wasn't much time before she'd be disconnected. She also had the feeling it was the last time she'd ever speak with her little sister.

"I'm fine. Listen, hon, what's today's date? The year and everything."

The answer came back promptly. Sounding bemused, Paula said, "August fourth, nineteen seventy-nine."

Good. She wasn't too late. Blinking back tears, Cindi said, "I love you so much, honey."

There was a pause and then her sister's words came, shy and sweet, over a distance of forty years. "I love you too."

There was a click, followed by the steady hum of the dial tone. Cindi put her head down and wept.

EVERYTHING HERE IS MINE

J.A.W. McCarthy

"Come alone," he pleaded, as if I were the same woman he knew back then, the same girl who couldn't go anywhere or do anything without encouragement and support. He thinks I can't still grow and change. He thinks I've stopped learning.

It's strange to see my house from the outside. "Your *old* home," he likes to remind me as exes do. Sometimes everything goes black and then I'm standing on the sidewalk or in the backyard, wedged between bushes and peering in the windows. Watching Jason in the living room, yet again furiously scrubbing at the smeared-soot letters above the fireplace while texting on his phone. Watching Alison in the kitchen, ballet flats balanced on a drawer handle so she can reach the cabinet above the refrigerator where her healthy supply of candles now lives. You don't know how many times, as her chin hovered above the edge of the refrigerator, I wished for that little bit of leather and satin to slip.

I left him everything. By default, really, but I would've done it on paper like that anyway. Almost every piece of furniture in that house is mine, came with me when we moved in. The couch and chairs and dining room set and my grandmother's roll-top desk by the window that overlooks the ravine where I used to watch the owls at night. Now Alison uses that desk as a craft table. A fucking craft table. She can't even scrapbook right.

The one that really gets me, though, is our bed. "The cradle of our marriage," Jason used to joke, hands folded in mock prayer and eyes to God just to make me laugh. I chose that bed and we bought it together, brand new, for us. Now Alison moans and grips the hand-carved headboard while he breathes her name into her hair the same way he used to breathe mine.

But it's just stuff. What am I going to do with all that furniture anyway? Even when Alison sneaks up to the attic and tries on my old dresses, I count to ten and then I let it go, as long as her hands are clean and she puts everything back in the wardrobe as she found it. Well, except for my wedding dress, which is also the red gingham halter dress I was wearing when Jason proposed to me on the overlook at the woods by our house. The last time Alison tried to put that dress on, the shelf above her collapsed. Jason found her minutes later under a stack of suitcases, clutching her head and cursing my name.

They're always cursing my name, so I write it everywhere every chance I get. I've used paint, markers, fireplace soot, and even raspberry jam. Once I burned my name in huge letters right above the bed as they slept. Alison screamed and checked into a hotel for the night after I did that. Jason actually cried.

The best one, though, was when Jason tripped over my books in the hallway. He went tumbling down the stairs and ended up with two black eyes. I must've laughed for a week straight.

So I'll come alone, as he requested. Not out of guilt or even a tiny shred of loyalty, but because I'm curious. I want to see them stubbornly, stupidly keep trying to play house. I want them to throw everything they have at me. I want them to see that I am stronger than they ever knew.

* * *

He keeps calling me. He's been doing it for days now, mostly him, but sometimes Alison calls out too. It starts all gentle and lilting like a lure, then moves to an insistent and firm "Laura!" as if I were a naughty pet that had just piddled on the rug. "Laura!" they bark when I don't answer, their mouths tight and their hands squeezing as they sit at the dining room table. Again, *my* dining room table. They're still calling right now because they don't know I'm already here.

It's after midnight and the only light comes from the circle of white pillar candles they've arranged on the dining room table. They sit opposite each other with their hands clasped across the surface, Alison jerking a little every time one of the flames jumps because she's afraid her sleeve will catch on fire. They both call for me again, their eyes raised cautiously to the ceiling, the uncertainty of horror movie recollections clear on their faces. The Jason I used to know would have set out the good plates and cooked my favorite pasta, welcomed me with bourbon instead of this bait-and-switch dinner party bullshit. My one-time friend Alison would've brought eclairs and cued up the playlist we used to dance to at her house. Now they both look like they're about to piss their pants. I'd like to see Alison scrapbook this little get-together.

"Okay, I'm here," I announce, settling into a seat between the two of them.

Alison drops Jason's hands, almost knocking over a candle as she slides her arms to brace at her sides. "Laura?"

"Uh, yeah."

"It's really you," Jason marvels, the whites of his eyes bright and perfectly round in the flickering light. "You came."

"You invited me," I sigh.

He leans towards me just as Alison is pushing back her seat. I hate the way he's staring at me, as if it's been so long that he can't trust his eyes, that if he blinks he might miss signs that I am an imposter. When he moves his hand towards me, I quickly pull my own hand off the table and into my lap.

"What's it like?" he starts. "Is there...Are you okay?"

"You have to stop!" Alison bursts.

Jason and I both look at her. She's got her chair pushed back as far as it will go and she's perched on the edge with her hands gripping the seat like she's buckled herself in for an earthquake. I loved her, but Jason and I used to laugh about how tightly wound she was, how she gripped the car door handle and winced every time we went above thirty.

"Ally, wait..."

"No!" she stands up abruptly, knocking her chair into the wall. "Laura, you have to stop it. You're scaring me. You're scaring us."

I expect Jason to go to her, but he doesn't. He just looks from her to me back and forth and says her name a couple more times in that condescending, soothing voice he used to use on me. If he calls her Ally Cat, I decide I will throw one of the lit candles at his head.

"Ally, she needs something from us." He turns to me for confirmation. "Laura, tell us, what do you need?"

"I need you to get a fucking grip."

Pressed against the wall, Alison's fingers roam to her throat and that's when I see it, the obsidian pendant nestled in the dip of her collarbone. The silver setting winks at me in the candlelight.

"Really?" I fume, rushing to her. I grab the pendant and pull the chain taut, twisting until our faces are just inches apart. "You had to take this? You have to take everything?"

Alison starts screaming and Jason is behind me now, trying to touch me again. No matter how hard he tries, though, he can't pull me back; I give him nothing to grip. As Alison blubbers "please" and "don't" and "stop" in jagged non sequiturs, I feel a halo around my vision, a narrowing that tunnels into the gold coming from her mouth. Behind me, Jason's murmuring starts to surface.

"Christ be with us, Christ be within us, I bind us unto the Name, the powerful Name of the Trinity…"

I toss the pendant back against Alison's collarbone and turn to Jason. "Are you serious? What is wrong with you?"

"Please, Laura. You can't keep doing this."

"You have to go," Alison agrees, rubbing the center of her throat.

"This isn't your home anymore, Laura."

I turn all the way around to face Jason. He takes a step back and I feel powerful in that moment, even more powerful than when I was writing my name on the walls and taking down shelves.

"Everything here is mine." I glance back at Alison. "You can't take it from me. You can't erase me."

"Please, Laura. You have to find peace. You have to give us peace."

There are tears streaking Alison's cheeks when she slips from behind me and joins Jason. They clasp hands and form a barricade in front of me, making me the one trapped against the wall now. When they start to chant, the halo returns and I feel myself falling back into nothing. Nothing to catch me, not even blackness. Just gold spreading everywhere.

"Christ be with us, Christ be within us, I bind us unto the Name, the powerful Name of the Trinity…"

"You've got to be fucking kidding me," is the last thing I remember saying.

* * *

There's a big empty spot where the bed should be, and at first I think I've somehow forgotten where the master bedroom is. Then I look up and I can see where they painted over my name, the dark burn of L-A-U-R-A only faded and now outlined in bright white. I'm surprised Alison hasn't attempted to decoupage over the spot.

They're calling me again, which makes no sense since they just tried to banish me five (ten? fifteen?) minutes ago. Time is hard for me to comprehend now; it moves like a small bird, pecking and hopping within reach, then soaring into the distance when I think I'm close enough to grasp it. I was falling back, then everything swirled into gold, and then I ended up here, in what used to be my favorite room. I used to sit by the window and rub lotion onto my legs in here – the best part of my morning – a prickle beneath my fingers as I inhaled the heady scent of cherry blossoms mingling with Jason's sweat from the night before. Now it smells like fake lemons in here, an empty cleanliness that's never allowed the residue of what flesh does in this room.

I hear Jason's footsteps weighing on the stairs, so I rush into the space that used to be all mine. It's Alison's now – she's made that clear by taking down my photos and filling the little closet with her tasteful cardigans and heels. Her puff-paint markers and fuzzy stickers and other craft supplies are gathered in a box that sits where my roll-top desk used to be. I unscrew all the lids on the little pots of glitter before Jason can get to me.

"Laura! I know you're still here. We just want to talk, okay? Please, let's just talk."

"We already talked," I answer, sliding past him in the hall.

I'm halfway down the stairs when I see it.

A sliver of white on the bottom step, a pearlescent spike the size of a fingernail clipping catching a little bit of moonlight from the open window. I pick it up, despite knowing right away what it is, and find comfort in its familiar smoothness. When I bend down again, I can see on the same step a cluster of three tiny teeth like kernels of corn cut from the cob.

"What the fuck is this?" I yell, holding up the tiny fang. I'm surprised that I can feel so hot, like everything is pulled tight and the burning is filling my head. Jason squints at me from the top of the stairs. "What did you do?" I demand.

This time I don't move when he approaches me. I stand firm, that tiny fang the only thing between us as he hovers on the step above me. I watch his eyes refuse to meet mine, his mouth opening and closing, and I brace myself for whatever weird religious chant is going to make everything slip around me again. Instead, after a sharp intake of breath, Jason does nothing more than look down at his feet.

"Look, I'm sorry, but we had to, okay? The things you're doing—"

"You killed her!"

"She died." He brings his hand to my shoulder as if he thinks he can console me; there is no satisfaction for either of us when his hand slides through the air. "She died," he repeats. "She was old. It was peaceful."

"You murdered her! The minute I'm gone, you just got rid of her too, you sick—"

"She died three years ago, Laura. Alison and I...we buried her in the backyard, under the laurel tree. We thought she'd be with you now."

Three years ago? I saw her last week, racing up and down the stairs like she used to. I felt her brush between my legs, her long black tail wrapping around my ankles.

"You buried her," I say, picturing Jason in the ratty shorts he always wore while doing yard work, Alison urging him to hurry up because she had dinner on the stove. I pinch the tiny fang between my fingers, willing it to pierce me. "Then you dug her up?"

"We had to. We've asked you – begged you – so many times. It's been almost four years, Laura. We can't go on like this anymore. What you're doing is cruel. It isn't fair. I know you're not happy."

The wall catches and holds me when I step back. It feels good, a cradle that reminds me of my physical form. The dining room is to my left and I can see little wisps of smoke from the blown-out candles still hanging in the air. Alison isn't there anymore.

Jason sits down on the second-to-the-last step, facing me. "You remember this?" he asks, running his finger down the bridge of his nose. "You broke my nose. You almost broke Alison's ankle last month."

The memory of Alison slipping all over the olive-oil-coated kitchen floor makes me smile. "It's not my fault she's clumsy."

"I still love you, Laura, but this isn't your home anymore. You have to go."

"This will always be my home."

"What about your grandmother? What about your friend Charlotte? Aren't they waiting for you?"

No one's waiting for me. I've been alone since the first day, the first minute, the first moment I realized that nothing inside of me moves or grows or exists anymore.

"Alison and I waited a long time after you. We really did. We don't deserve this. I was willing to live with you, but…you're going to kill us."

There are dark edges gathering around my face, breaking apart and bleeding into me like ink on rag paper. I can hear Jason still blathering on about how nothing can replace me even though he loves Alison now, but his voice keeps falling backwards into the static of crickets and tires and the earth shifting beneath us. Everything is alive out there, and they have places where they belong and places where they can go. Tomorrow Jason will bring Alison coffee in bed and they will argue about what movie to see, and they will eat dinner on the patio and get drinks at the French bar I used to like. Meanwhile, the darkness will continue to bleed into me, knitting together until one day that's all there will be. I look down at my cat's fang in my palm one last time, then press it into the center of my chest, relaxing as whatever I am now absorbs it.

As I go, Jason's voice suddenly rises above the stifling hum. He's calling me again. I like the way he's saying my name.

* * *

Jason and Alison are waiting for me in the backyard. Between them, piled in a tidy pyramid on the lawn, are the things I am missing: our bed, my grandmother's roll-top desk, my favorite books, my cat's bones laid out on my red gingham dress. Everything that is mine.

Alison is standing very stiffly, as if she's holding her breath, a small metal canister in her hand. She looks to Jason, then back to me. "You do not belong here, Laura. This is not your home anymore. These are not your things." Even her words sound rehearsed.

I turn to Jason, my middle seizing as my mouth splits in laughter. It sounds so loud to me, like I might wake the neighbors, but he doesn't look particularly alarmed or amused. Behind him and his new wife, the moon highlights brittle branches like loose blonde hairs knotted over the ravine.

"Is that holy water?" I ask, pointing to Alison. The laugher comes in hiccups. "Where's your crucifix? Don't tell me you couldn't get a priest to come out."

Jason stiffens, takes a step forward that Alison mirrors. "You do not belong here, Laura. This is not your home anymore. These are not your things."

"Jesus, you two have a script?"

"Laura, we have been fair and we have been respectful. We have asked and you have not complied. In His name and the name of the Trinity, Laura, we banish you from this house and this land. Laura, we command that you move on to where you belong."

They chant it together over and over again until the words lose all melody and meaning and become a strange jumble of animal sounds against my ears. Even my name – Laura – is worn and flattened until it's nothing more than the bellow of a cow. I would still be laughing if it wasn't for the dark, leaking edges forming around my vision once more. Every time they say "Trinity" it's like a bell, like the *ding* of a timer that makes the gold pour from their mouths. They are throbbing in front of me, and I wish I could feel the cold they appear to be stoically steeling themselves against. Still chanting, Alison takes off my obsidian necklace and tosses it atop my grandmother's roll-top desk. She starts to circle all of my things, shaking her small metal canister over the pile. I watch as my red gingham dress deflates and my cat's bones glisten under the lighter fluid.

"You two are sick!" I cry.

Jason stops chanting and walks towards me as Alison

drones on in the background. "This is your last chance, Laura. If you go now, of your own free will, we don't have to do this. We don't have to send you to that place." Even in the dark, his eyes glow, shiny with cheap tears and real, sincere pity.

"You can't do this!" I yell over Alison. "This is mine! You can't take it from me!"

Nodding to Alison, Jason returns to his spot on the other side of the pile. I watch as they each whip out a matchbook and strike little flames in unison.

"Last chance!" he calls.

"Fuck you both!"

The endless loop of their chanting never changes pitch, despite the sudden flash that spreads into a hundred fingers of fire reaching out from all of my things; Alison manages to stay on beat even when she is forced to jump back from a rogue flame. The silky orange mixes with the gold from their mouths as they move to one side of the burning pile and join hands. The bellow of my name becomes a hammer – *comply LAURA, banish LAURA, move on LAURA* – and everything is buckling and shrinking, all that's left of me curled and sinking into the grass. My dress, gone like paper. My bed, hobbled to three then two legs like a horse kneeling. My beautiful little fangs going flat then black. I am reaching into the fire, but my arms fall outside the halo. The edges grow darker and darker, just undulating orange at the end of the tunnel. When I turn my head, I catch a glimpse of the intricately tiled grave marker under the laurel tree, her name spelled out in colorful stones below her picture. I hate to admit it, but it's beautiful.

The gold is overtaken by the orange. It pulls me in,

tucking me into my place alongside what used to be mine, the linked bodies and words of the people I used to love erasing me. Consuming me.

* * *

The darkness, like before, is nothing – just the space between blinks – because I am learning to interpret time now. Everything that is mine is still burning. The dark sky is flecked with floating ash, its brown middle an umbrella over the pulsating orange bottom. I think of the fire as a living thing, leaping and reaching and growing and driving them away. Doing the things I can't, for me.

The fire follows me. Skipping across the lawn, spitting onto the roof, it adorns every shingle and hinge until the whole house is ablaze. All of my burning remnants give me strength. I spread the flames they create across the back porch, then the wooden fence, then the trees. Jason and Alison are backing away in shock, their eyes and mouths wide dark voids as they yell to me, but I keep racing my flames towards them. Their words do nothing, mean nothing.

Broken noses and black eyes were just an outlet, my way of expressing what I couldn't before. I admit I have been spiteful. I admit I've been enjoying the power I have found. I bathe every uncovered inch in fire, and Jason and Alison stumble, and Jason drops his phone, and they start to run. My reach is long. I could end them.

Instead, I let them run into the ravine.

They will come back, of course. Tomorrow they'll come back, decide it's too much, and settle somewhere else. After the firemen come and there is nothing left but singed earth and wet ash, I will still be here. When what's left goes to rot and the earth grows its new skin and strangers come and build, I will still be where I belong.

This brittle, disintegrating husk is your old home now, Jason. This land, this place, will always be mine.

AUTHOR BIOGRAPHIES

These are printed in alphabetical order by contributor surname.

Phillip Drake

Even as a young child, Phillip Drake was always conjuring up stories, filling them with colourful characters and sharing them with anyone and everyone who would listen. Since then, he has progressed to longer, more complex works and sharing them with a wider audience. He is the author of several books including *To Be a Saint*, chronicling his avid fanship of Southampton Football Club, and *Dark Window*, a collection of horror short stories. You'll find his story "Mr Cruel" included in *The Second Corona Book of Horror Stories*, and he has just finished work on his latest non-fiction book, *Hell of a Season: The Worst Campaigns in English Football History*, which will be available soon.

Sue (J.) Eaton

Sue J. Eaton and Sue Eaton are one and the same person, editor of this volume and writer of short stories herself.

As a girl growing up in Northamptonshire, she became fascinated by the work of authors such as Ray Bradbury, John Wyndham and Terry Nation, developing a lifelong love for a well-written psychological horror story. She worked for many years as a teacher of children with autism. Her writing is now one of her major passions. She has had her work broadcast on BBC Radio 4 and her debut novel, *The Woman Who Was Not His Wife*, was published in 2018.

Angelique Fawns

Angelique Fawns is a journalist and television producer, writer and editor. She began her career writing about naked cave dwellers in Tenerife and parasailing in Australia, and now works for Global TV in Toronto. She lives on a farm with her husband, daughter, cows, horses, fainting goats and an attack llama. On 27th May 2018 she tripped over her Cane Corso Bulldog Pansy and broke her ankle. This sat her in a chair for three months with a cast on, but finally gave her time to pursue her dream of becoming the next Stephen King or Anne Rice. Her dark fiction has already been published in literary reviews and *Ellery Queen Mystery Magazine*.

Matthew Gorman

Matthew Gorman lives in Seattle, Washington, where he writes horror and other speculative fiction, and surrounds himself with what he calls a collection of oddities. He's an active member of several horror writers' groups and his work has appeared in a number of anthologies, including most recently HorrorTree.com's first print release,

Trembling with Fear: Year One. He's a huge fan of classic horror in the vein of Edgar Allan Poe, H.P. Lovecraft and Robert W. Chambers, as well as being a steadfast acolyte of the modern classics.

Donna L. Greenwood

Donna L. Greenwood describes herself as a daydreamer, unashamed idealist and writer of weird stuff. Her flash fiction, short stories and poetry have been published by the likes of *STORGY Magazine*, *The Airgonaut* and *EllipsisZine*. Her story "The Night of the Last Dreams" recently won first prize in *The Molotov Cocktail*'s Flash Legends competition, and her "We Are All Alone When the Dark Comes" won Horror Scribes' Trapped Flash competition. She lives in Lancashire, England, in which county her story here, "Amy", is set.

Ali Habashi

Ali Habashi graduated from the University of St Andrews, Scotland with a degree in English and Management, and currently works in Boston, Massachusetts for an academic publisher. When not at work, she can usually be found drinking coffee and stressing about a self-inflicted creative project involving monsters or witches. Her short stories have been featured several times on The Other Stories horror podcast (Hawk and Cleaver) and appear in print in the likes of the Transmundane Press anthology *Transcendence*. She also came first in the Creature Feature category for *The Asterisk Anthology Vol II*.

Jill Hand

Jill Hand is a former newspaper reporter and editor from New Jersey, whose writing is occasionally inspired by her belief that everyone is a little bit crazy in one way or another. She is a member of both the Horror Writers Association and International Thriller Writers. Her short stories have appeared in many anthologies, including *Mrs Rochester's Attic*, *Postcards from the Void* and *Test Patterns*. Her time-travel novella *The Blue Horse* won a Pinnacle Book Award for fantasy and science fiction. Her first full-length thriller, the Southern Gothic novel *White Oaks,* was published by Black Rose Writing in 2019.

Eryn Hiscock

Eryn Hiscock lives and writes in North York, Ontario. Her work has been published online and in various literary journals and anthologies across Canada and the U.S. Her writing takes in poetry as well as speculative fiction, with her poems having been published in the magazines *Descant, Room* and *OnSpec.* She is typically at work on more than one project at a time and is trying to figure out how to get Superman to reverse the rotation of the Earth for a few hours each day to buy herself more writing time.

J.A.W. McCarthy

J.A.W. McCarthy goes by Jen when she is not writing. She lives with her husband and assistant cat in the Pacific Northwest, a place that inspires her dark tales. Besides writing, she enjoys reading and yelling at the TV, often at the same time. She is a member of the Horror Writers Association. Her work has appeared in numerous publications, including *Transcendent*, *She's Lost Control*, *Nightscript*, *Vastarien* and Flame Tree Publishing's *Lost Souls*.

John Mueter

John Mueter is an educator, composer, pianist/accompanist and vocal coach – and a writer of short fiction. His stories have appeared in numerous journals and anthologies, including *American Athenaeum*, *Lowestoft Chronicle*, *Halfway Down the Stairs*, *Bibliotheca Alexandrina*, *The Literary Nest* and *The First Line*.

Jude Reid

Jude Reid is a Scottish horror writer, whose recent work includes co-writing *Tales from the Aletheian Society,* a serialised comedy-horror audio drama about the misadventures of a society of Victorian occultists. She and her co-writer Christopher Edwards have a long history of creating exciting worlds together, having written and organised a series of highly successful LARP events, including Project Ragnarok and Incarceration. Jude is also one of the team of writers behind the forthcoming Novitero Podcast.

C.E. Rickard

Catherine Rickard grew up in the small, rural village of Chinnor, Oxfordshire. She began writing short stories and poetry as a young child, incorporating her love of the countryside and all things supernatural into her writing even then. At 39, she was diagnosed with the eye condition Retinitis Pigmentosa. Her gradually failing sight provided the spur she needed to make her take her writing ambitions more seriously. "Every cloud…" as she puts it. To date she has had a number of her short stories published and is completing work on her debut novel, the supernatural thriller *The Brayford Witch*.

C.M. Saunders

Christian Saunders is a freelance journalist and editor from South Wales. His work has appeared in over 80 anthologies, e-zines and magazines worldwide, including the likes of *Loaded, Maxim, Record Collector* and *Fortean Times*. He has held staff positions at several leading UK magazines ranging from Staff Writer to Associate Editor. His books have been both traditionally and independently published, the latest release being *X:Omnibus*, which gathers all his short stories to date into one bumper volume. When he's not writing, he plays snooker very badly and supports Cardiff City F.C. very well.

Mike Sherer

Mike Sherer lives in West Chester in the Greater Cincinnati area of Ohio and has written fiction in different forms his entire life, including short stories, novellas, stage plays and screenplays and latterly blogs. His screenplay "Hamal_18", about a detective who assumes the persona of his young daughter and obsessively hunts internet chat rooms for the paedophile who killed her, was produced as an independent film in

Los Angeles, and the movie is currently available to watch/buy on Amazon or to rent at Netflix DVD. Mike is also the author of the mystery/fantasy novel *A Cold Dish* published by James Ward Kirk Fiction, along with numerous published novellas and short stories.

Phillip Tomasso

Phillip Tomasso is the award-winning author of 26 novels, including the crime novel *You Choose* and the supernatural thriller *Woman in the Woods*. His books cover a wide variety of genres, including horror, young adult, science fiction, and fantasy. With "Jenny" he returns to his first love of writing short stories – he started his writing career that way. When not writing, Phillip works as a Fire/EMS Dispatcher for 9-1-1. He works the midnight shift and finds the hours conducive to his creativity. He lives in Rochester, New York with his three kids – who are not little any longer. He is always at work on a next novel.

Christopher Wilson

Christopher Wilson lives in Ontario, Canada, with his wife, daughter and their dog Luna. A lifelong storyteller, Christopher only recently started submitting his work for publication. "The Walking Woman" is his first short story to be published, but it will be quickly followed by another that has also been accepted for publication and will be included in Blood Bound Books' *Crash Code* anthology.

AUTHOR WEBSITES AND TWITTER ACCOUNTS

Those authors who have Twitter accounts and/or their own websites are listed below. All of them will welcome website visits and you following them on Twitter, and you will be rewarded with some other great writing.

Phillip Drake

Twitter: @pdrakeofficial
website: phildrakeauthor.wixsite.com/website

Sue Eaton

Twitter: @SueJayEaton
website: susanjeaton.com

Angelique Fawns

Twitter: @ Raingirl51
website: fawns.ca

Donna L. Greenwood

Twitter: @DonnaLouise67
website: thehorrorsblog.wordpress.com

Ali Habashi

website: alihabashi.com

Jill Hand

Twitter: @jillhand1_gef
website: jillhandauthor.com

J.A.W. McCarthy

website: jawmccarthy.com

John Mueter

website: johnmueter.wordpress.com

C.M. Saunders

Twitter: @CMSaunders01
website: cmsaunders.wordpress.com

Mike Sherer

Twitter: @mikewsherer
website: mikesherer.org

Phillip Tomasso

Twitter: @P_Tomasso
website: philliptomasso.com

CORONA BOOKS

Innovative, brilliant and quirky

Corona Books UK is an independent publishing company, newly established in 2015. We aim to publish the brilliant, innovative and quirky, regardless of genre. That said, we do have a fondness for sci-fi and horror!

For the latest on other titles published by us and forthcoming attractions, please visit our website and follow us on Twitter.

www.coronabooks.com

@CoronaBooksUK

Readers who enjoyed the stories by Phillip Drake and Sue Eaton may especially be interested in *The Second Corona Book of Horror Stories*, which includes stories from both these authors. Stories by Sue Eaton are also included in other Corona Books anthologies and her debut novel, the sci-fi thriller *The Woman Who Was Not His Wife*, is also available.